D1549398

LOVE FINDS THE DUKE AT LAST

As they moved down the passage, Devinia put her hand on his arm.

"Please don't let what has happened spoil you," she said. "Mama always said when things went wrong we were to pray that the sun would shine tomorrow and we would forget very quickly that we had been hurt or that people had been unkind."

"Your mother was so right," he agreed. "You and I will make a vow here and now that we will not think of the past or keep referring to why we have had to come here."

He paused before he carried on,

"We will just enjoy ourselves hour by hour and day by day until all that is wrong and unpleasant fades into the past and we forget about it."

Devinia clapped her hands and gave a jump of joy.

"That is just what I wanted you to say!" she cried. "This house is beautiful and everything in it is so perfect, I could not bear you and I to spoil it by talking about the things that have made us unhappy."

She thought to herself as she spoke that she must not mourn Jo-Jo and once again the Duke had shown his kindness to her by producing another dog for her.

THE BARBARA CARTLAND PINK COLLECTION

Titles in this series

1. The Cross Of Love
2. Love In The Highlands
3. Love Finds The Way
4. The Castle Of Love
5. Love Is Triumphant
6. Stars In The Sky
7. The Ship Of Love
8. A Dangerous Disguise
9. Love Became Theirs
10. Love Drives In
11. Sailing To Love
12. The Star Of Love
13. Music Is The Soul Of Love
14. Love In The East
15. Theirs To Eternity
16. A Paradise On Earth
17. Love Wins In Berlin
18. In Search Of Love
19. Love Rescues Rosanna
20. A Heart In Heaven
21. The House Of Happiness
22. Royalty Defeated By Love
23. The White Witch
24. They Sought Love
25. Love Is The Reason For Living
26. They Found Their Way To Heaven
27. Learning To Love
28. Journey To Happiness
29. A Kiss In The Desert
30. The Heart Of Love
31. The Richness Of Love
32. For Ever And Ever
33. An Unexpected Love
34. Saved By An Angel
35. Touching The Stars
36. Seeking Love
37. Journey To Love
38. The Importance Of Love
39. Love By The Lake
40. A Dream Come True
41. The King Without A Heart
42. The Waters Of Love
43. Danger To The Duke
44. A Perfect Way To Heaven
45. Follow Your Heart
46. In Hiding
47. Rivals For Love
48. A Kiss From The Heart
49. Lovers In London
50. This Way To Heaven
51. A Princess Prays
52. Mine For Ever
53. The Earl's Revenge
54. Love At The Tower
55. Ruled By Love
56. Love Came From Heaven
57. Love And Apollo
58. The Keys Of Love
59. A Castle Of Dreams
60. A Battle Of Brains
61. A Change Of Hearts
62. It Is Love
63. The Triumph Of Love
64. Wanted – A Royal Wife
65. A Kiss Of Love
66. To Heaven With Love
67. Pray For Love
68. The Marquis Is Trapped
69. Hide And Seek For Love
70. Hiding From Love
71. A Teacher Of Love
72. Money Or Love
73. The Revelation Is Love
74. The Tree Of Love
75. The Magnificent Marquis
76. The Castle
77. The Gates Of Paradise
78. A Lucky Star
79. A Heaven On Earth
80. The Healing Hand
81. A Virgin Bride
82. The Trail To Love
83. A Royal Love Match
84. A Steeplechase For Love
85. Love At Last
86. Search For A Wife
87. Secret Love
88. A Miracle Of Love
89. Love And The Clans
90. A Shooting Star
91. The Winning Post Is Love
92. They Touched Heaven
93. The Mountain Of Love
94. The Queen Wins
95. Love And The Gods
96. Joined By Love
97. The Duke Is Deceived
98. A Prayer For Love
99. Love Conquers War
100. A Rose In Jeopardy
101. A Call Of Love
102. A Flight To Heaven
103. She Wanted Love
104. A Heart Finds Love
105. A Sacrifice For Love
106. Love's Dream In Peril
107. Soft, Sweet And Gentle
108. An Archangel Called Ivan
109. A Prisoner In Paris
110. Danger In The Desert
111. Rescued By Love
112. A Road To Romance
113. A Golden Lie
114. A Heart Of Stone
115. The Earl Elopes
116. A Wilder Kind Of Love
117. The Bride Runs Away
118. Beyond The Horizon
119. Crowned By Music
120. Love Solves The Problem
121. Blessing Of The Gods
122. Love By Moonlight
123. Saved By The Duke
124. A Train To Love
125. Wanted – A Bride
126. Double The Love
127. Hiding From The Fortune-Hunters
128. The Marquis Is Deceived
129. The Viscount's Revenge
130. Captured By Love
131. An Ocean Of Love
132. A Beauty Betrayed
133. No Bride, No Wedding
134. A Strange Way To Find Love
135. The Unbroken Dream
136. A Heart In Chains
137. One Minute To Love
138. Love For Eternity
139. The Prince Who Wanted Love
140. For The Love Of Scotland
141. An Angel From Heaven
142. Their Search For Real Love
143. Secret Danger
144. Music From Heaven
145. The Duke Hated Women
146. The Weapon Is Love
147. The King Wins
148. Love Saves The Day
149. They Ran Away
150. A Battle Of Love
151. Love Finds A Treasure
152. Love Under The Stars
153. She Fell In Love
154. The Earl In Peril
155. Love Cannot Fail
156. Love Has No Name
157. A Princess Runs Away
158. From The Dangers Of Russia To Love
159. Love Danced In
160. Love Finds The Duke At Last

LOVE FINDS THE DUKE AT LAST

BARBARA CARTLAND

Barbaracartland.com Ltd

THE BARBARA CARTLAND PINK COLLECTION

Dame Barbara Cartland is still regarded as the most prolific bestselling author in the history of the world.

In her lifetime she was frequently in the Guinness Book of Records for writing more books than any other living author.

Her most amazing literary feat was to double her output from 10 books a year to over 20 books a year when she was 77 to meet the huge demand.

She went on writing continuously at this rate for 20 years and wrote her very last book at the age of 97, thus completing an incredible 400 books between the ages of 77 and 97.

Her publishers finally could not keep up with this phenomenal output, so at her death in 2000 she left behind an amazing 160 unpublished manuscripts, something that no other author has ever achieved.

Barbara's son, Ian McCorquodale, together with his daughter Iona, felt that it was their sacred duty to publish all these titles for Barbara's millions of admirers all over the world who so love her wonderful romances.

So in 2004 they started publishing the 160 brand new Barbara Cartlands as *The Barbara Cartland Pink Collection*, as Barbara's favourite colour was always pink – and yet more pink!

The Barbara Cartland Pink Collection is published monthly exclusively by Barbaracartland.com and the books are numbered in sequence from 1 to 160.

Enjoy receiving a brand new Barbara Cartland book each month by taking out an annual subscription to the Pink Collection, or purchase the books individually.

The Pink Collection is available from the Barbara Cartland website www.barbaracartland.com via mail order and through all good bookshops.

In addition Ian and Iona are proud to announce that The Barbara Cartland Pink Collection is now available in ebook format as from Valentine's Day 2011.

For more information, please contact us at:

Barbaracartland.com Ltd.
Camfield Place
Hatfield
Hertfordshire AL9 6JE
United Kingdom

Telephone: +44 (0)1707 642629
Fax: +44 (0)1707 663041
Email: info@barbaracartland.com

THE LATE DAME BARBARA CARTLAND

Barbara Cartland who sadly died in May 2000 at the age of nearly 99 was the world's most famous romantic novelist who wrote 723 books in her lifetime with worldwide sales of over 1 billion copies and her books were translated into 36 different languages.

As well as romantic novels, she wrote historical biographies, 6 autobiographies, theatrical plays, books of advice on life, love, vitamins and cookery. She also found time to be a political speaker and television and radio personality.

She wrote her first book at the age of 21 and this was called *Jigsaw*. It became an immediate bestseller and sold 100,000 copies in hardback and was translated into 6 different languages. She wrote continuously throughout her life, writing bestsellers for an astonishing 76 years. Her books have always been immensely popular in the United States, where in 1976 her current books were at numbers 1 & 2 in the B. Dalton bestsellers list, a feat never achieved before or since by any author.

Barbara Cartland became a legend in her own lifetime and will be best remembered for her wonderful romantic novels, so loved by her millions of readers throughout the world.

Her books will always be treasured for their moral message, her pure and innocent heroines, her good looking and dashing heroes and above all her belief that the power of love is more important than anything else in everyone's life.

"All of us are seeking something or someone really special and unique in our lives and the word that comes so readily to mind is 'love'. My advice has always been never look for love because you will find love in the most unexpected places and by what will seem pure chance. And you will be happy ever after."

Barbara Cartland

CHAPTER ONE
1901

The Duke of Lavenham walked slowly downstairs to the breakfast room.

His breakfast had been ready for him for quite some time, but he had come home very late from a party which had been extremely amusing.

Contrary to his usual rules he had stayed nearly to the end.

He then sat down at the head of the breakfast table which overlooked the garden at the back of his gracious house in Park Lane in the middle of Mayfair, the smartest district in London.

His large dining room had a view of Hyde Park, but his breakfast room which was very much smaller and not so impressive caught the early morning sunshine streaming in through the windows which he greatly appreciated.

The butler and two footmen hurried to bring in the dishes, which were cooked and ready for him. As well as the special tea from India he always drank at breakfast.

As he disliked conversation early in the morning, the servants did not speak to him and he did not speak to them.

After he had sat down at the table, he saw with a sigh that there was a large pile of private letters which his secretary had put ready for him by his place.

Anything that was a bill or of an official nature was opened by his secretary and he saw them later in the day. But his private letters were placed on the breakfast table.

He gazed at them for a short while and thought that he recognised the handwriting on at least three of them.

At the age of twenty-eight the Duke of Lavenham was at his best and exceedingly handsome.

More than one beauty had complained to him,

"It is unfair that you should be so good-looking as well as so rich and a Duke. You have too much and who can compete with you?"

The Duke had laughed heartily at the time and had then dismissed the remark with a sardonic twist of his lips and the beauty had left his side looking embarrassed.

But he often thought that he was exceedingly lucky.

His father had always been short of money until he had married an heiress and so the family fortunes had then soared upwards.

What was more, the present Duke had been left a considerable amount of money by one of his Godparents.

"You are indeed the luckiest man in the world," several of his friends had told him and he had not disagreed with them.

In fact he was exceedingly grateful to Fate that had made him, unlike a number of his contemporaries, not have to worry continually over money and have, as he had often been told, creditors constantly knocking at their doors.

The daily newspapers were by his side at the table arranged on a silver holder, which put them exactly at the right angle for him to read them at the same time as he ate his breakfast.

There was not much news in any of them and what there was seemed rather boring and uninteresting.

He therefore pushed the newspapers to one side and finished the excellent dish of salmon kedgeree that he was eating and then stretched out his hand for the first letter.

It was from an old friend who he had taken out two nights ago, who had now left London. She wrote to say how much she had enjoyed seeing him again and thanked him for a most entertaining evening.

"*You must come and stay with us as soon as you can spare the time,*" she wrote. "*Arthur is longing to see your new horses and I think you will be quite envious of two he has bought recently.*"

She ended with some complimentary words about his appearance and several words of love which he knew were true.

He was very fond of her and, if she had not been married when they first met, he often thought that he might well have asked her to marry him.

But she was very happy with her husband and now had three charming children and the Duke was a Godfather to the youngest.

He then put the letter on one side and opened the next one. For a moment he could not guess who it was from although the handwriting was somewhat familiar.

Then when he opened it he realised that it was from his cousin, Lady Western, who he saw as little as possible.

The reason for this was because she was the biggest gossip in his family.

They all knew that if they ever told her anything, however secret it may be, it was repeated over and over again to all the rest of their relations and to her friends.

The Duke wondered why she was writing to him and he was certain that it would not be anything he wanted to hear.

At the same time it would be a mistake to quarrel with her simply because everyone in the family would be aware of it immediately.

He then gave a sigh as he took the letter out of the envelope and commenced reading it.

He was quite certain that he would be told the latest scandal about one of his relations or else be reprimanded as she invariably did, because he had ignored someone who had once been friends of his father or his mother who had come to London without, as had often happened, being entertained by him.

As if to fortify himself he drank a sip of his tea.

Then he was aware that it was not one letter he had taken from the envelope but two.

Without being curious as to why it was there, he started to read the letter from Muriel which began,

"Dearest Ivan,

My daughter, Charlotte, has received the enclosed letter this morning from her friend, Penelope Denton.

They were at school together and have been great friends ever since. In fact Penelope has often stayed here with us, although I never liked her.

Nor did I think that she was a particularly good person for Charlotte to have as a friend.

However, they have been good friends ever since and Charlotte often goes to stay with her for some festivity or another.

I am, however, shocked at the letter she received this morning and I think you should read it.

I am enclosing it for you to do so.

With fondest love,

Your affectionate cousin,

Muriel."

The Duke was frowning when he finished reading his cousin's letter.

Then he opened the letter tucked inside hers.

He realised that it was from someone he had been spending a great deal of his time with, who he had found exciting and amusing as well as being one of the most fêted and admired social beauties in the whole of London.

He frowned again as he read,

"Dearest Charlotte,

I have won! I have won! You will hardly believe it, but I told you I would do so.

The evasive Duke is on the verge of asking me to marry him and, of course, I will fall into his arms and say, 'yes, yes, yes!'

You therefore owe me five pounds, as I told you I would marry a Duke and you told me that it was just impossible to capture one.

But I have done it, despite all the difficulties which we all know has made him elude so many traps and then manage to remain single and his own Master despite the allurement that has always surrounded him.

It is now only a question of time until he will say the words I want to hear and then I will march up the aisle triumphant as soon as possible just in case he changes his mind at the last moment.

It is now up to you, my dear, to capture, at the very least, a Marquis or an Earl!

But, in any case, you still owe me five pounds and I also expect a magnificent Wedding present from you.

You were always positive that I would never land a Duke as I intended to do, but I have done it and I can assure you that I will be a fantastic Duchess and my tiara, at the State Opening of Parliament, will be larger and better than anyone else's.

Do not please tell any of my family about this until the announcement is actually in the newspapers.

I want to surprise everyone and I am exceedingly pleased with myself that, as I said to you all that time ago at school, I would marry a Duke whatever he was like and however much he tried to evade me.

As I have always got my own way, I wanted you to be the first to know that I have won my bet and, as you can imagine, I am very pleased with myself.

With so much love and please tear this letter up as soon as you have read it.

Yours

Penelope."

As the Duke read the letter, his eyes hardened and there was an expression on his face that those who served him knew was restrained anger.

Because he was very proud of himself and his title, the Duke never raised his voice when he was angry. Nor did he when he had to reprimand a servant or someone who had offended him.

Yet they were well aware of his anger and few men or women made any attempt to retaliate.

He had in fact been on the very edge of proposing marriage to Penelope simply because she was so beautiful and her special loveliness was duly acclaimed by everyone.

Not only would their Wedding be the smartest and most spectacular Wedding of the year, but he would be the envy of all his male friends.

Yet beneath this there was something else which to him was of tremendous importance.

Ever since he had left Eton he had been pressured to marry because of his elevated social position and he was an exceedingly charming and gracious gentleman.

Equally he knew that it was his title which dazzled the young women around him like a star in the sky.

As his mother had once said to him,

"Every young woman as she grows up hopes and prays that one day a Duke or an Earl will drop down the chimney. He will be young, handsome and charming and she will love him with all her heart. Their marriage will be as happy as your father's and mine has been."

His mother had gone on to tell him that they had fallen in love with each other the moment they met.

He had not been a Duke then, but, of course, he was the eldest son of one.

But that did not matter.

"In some extraordinary way when he first walked into the room where I was, I just felt my heart turn a total somersault," his mother had told him. "Your father said exactly the same thing happened to him. The moment he saw me he knew that I was the girl he had been looking for and had never found."

If his mother had told him the story once, she had told it to him many times.

As he grew older the Duke was well aware that the invitations he received and the compliments that were paid him were really directed more to his title than to himself.

It was around then that he became suspicious of the ambitious mothers with pretty daughters who pressed him to accept their endless invitations.

The daughters themselves would he always felt fall into his arms if he just put his hand out towards them.

When his father had died and he became the Duke of Lavenham, he realised all too clearly just how much in demand he was in English Society because of his title and not particularly because of himself.

It was actually not only individuals who wanted his attention, it was Companies, Charities and organisations of every kind who craved his patronage.

It was just impossible for him not to become rather blasé and at the same time suspicious.

When women gushed at him, he was almost certain that they were thinking of his title, riches and possessions rather than himself.

He was conscious that every ambitious Dowager in the Social world wanted to hand him to their daughter as if she was on a plate.

It was then he made a vow to himself that he would never marry unless the woman he asked to do so loved him for himself.

But even as he thought about it he knew that it would be the most difficult thing in the world to find.

Yet he thought now that he had been almost trapped when he least expected it.

As Penelope was such a shining star in the Social world and had always had every man at her feet, he had thought the way she looked at him was different from what he had encountered before.

He felt that what she really was offering him was her heart.

It had been impossible for him not to be delighted that she obviously preferred him to any of the other men who constantly surrounded her.

Quite a number of them were almost as important as he was and one man in particular would finally become a Duke when his cousin, who had produced no direct heir, died.

It must have been after he had kissed her one night in the Conservatory of the house they were both attending a ball in, that the words, '*will you marry me*' quivered on his lips, as he took them from hers.

Then, just as he was about to speak, the dance must have finished and several other people, talking loudly and laughing, came bursting into the Conservatory.

The Duke and Penelope were too late to move away and then it was impossible for them not to welcome the intruders as they joined them.

When they went back to the ballroom together, the Duke found that he could not take Penelope away from the throng of ardent admirers who surrounded her.

Only when they eventually said 'goodnight' to each other as her mother wished to leave, did Penelope say in a low voice, so that only he could hear,

"Come and see me tomorrow."

She had looked up into his eyes as she had spoken.

And he thought with a throb in his heart that she undoubtedly loved him as he loved her.

The Duke was feeling tired when he reached home and was ready for his bed.

Although he thought that he would stay awake all night thinking about Penelope, he had slept deeply without dreaming until his valet came into his room and drew back the curtains.

Now, having read the letter, he felt as if the sun had ceased to shine and he was in a darkness which was all too familiar.

He had been unable to visit Penelope the day after the ball for the simple reason that, when he got home, he found out that he had promised to make a speech at a very prestigious luncheon party that was taking place in the City of Maidstone.

It meant he had to leave as soon as he was dressed and, as the luncheon party was followed by a meeting at which he was the Chairman, he did not return to London until it was nearly dark.

His secretary, on his instructions, had sent Penelope a large bouquet of spring flowers.

He had not written her a letter and knew with a twist of his lips that her rooms in her father's and mother's house were filled with endless bouquets of every sort and description from her many admirers.

*

When he woke in the morning, he had thought that he had only one engagement of any consequence and at three o'clock he could easily leave for Penelope's parents' house which was on the outskirts of London.

As Penelope was such a success, they had rented a large house near Hampton Court.

"It will be very easy for us to hold dances in the ballroom," her mother had said, "and it will be far easier to entertain in what is more or less in the countryside than be confined in a house in London which will not have a big enough garden and people will complain that they cannot find proper accommodation for their horses and grooms."

The Duke had actually found this to be true.

When he went to Penelope's house, his grooms said that the accommodation for the horses was very different from what they had to put up with in London.

'I can easily be there in time for tea,' the Duke told himself. 'As they will then undoubtedly ask me to stay for dinner, I can talk to Penelope afterwards.'

Now he thought, when he read the letter again, that he had been made a fool of in exactly the same way as his friends he had been at school with were now suffering.

He knew of at least three of them who had been married for their titles rather than for themselves.

They had informed him on various occasions how unhappy they were and how, if they had their schooldays over again, they would be very careful who they married and would make quite certain that the woman loved him for himself and not for his social eminence.

One man, who was a Marquis, had told him several times how unhappy he was and how he would like to have a divorce.

"But you know as well as I do," he had said to the Duke, "that it will not only make my family miserable but be a bad example to the young boys who are growing up and who will be pursued in the same way as we were."

There had been a long pause and, as the Duke said nothing, the Marquis had added,

"When my wife fights with me in front of them and makes it obvious that she is not interested in me as a man, I hope that they are learning the lessons that we should have learnt and gone on searching for the woman who wants her husband as a man not as a figurehead."

He had spoken bitterly and the Duke knew that he was extremely unhappy with a wife who constantly found fault with him and contradicted him in public.

'I would not be such a fool,' he had said to himself at the time.

Yet now he had been on the very verge of it.

Then he asked himself what he should do to make Penelope fully aware that she had not captured him as she thought she had.

Without thinking he had promised to see her the next day after the party and it was only when he got home that he remembered that it was something he could not do.

He therefore told his secretary to send his apologies to Penelope's father and mother saying that he could not come as he hoped to do, but that he would certainly call to see them at teatime the following day.

It passed through his mind that he should send a servant with more apologies that he could not come today.

Then he thought that she would still be thinking of perhaps writing to even more of her friends to say that she had caught him *hook, line and sinker*.

And they would therefore be expecting an official announcement of their engagement at any moment.

'What I must do,' he determined, 'is to go there and make it very clear to Penelope that a kiss is just a kiss and nothing of any significance and that I have no intention at the moment of marrying anyone, least of all her!'

As the thought spread over him, he felt himself rage with anger that he himself had been just so stupid and so foolish in believing that she cared for him as a man.

'I will make her realise that I have no intention of marrying,' he thought. 'After all I only kissed her and I am quite sure that Penelope has kissed many men, but had no intention of marching up the aisle with any of them.'

He very nearly laughed out loud to himself as his thoughts continued.

'It is me she wants because I happen to be a Duke, not because I am a man and not because I am someone she loves and who loves her.'

Because he had always been most self-controlled, he merely sat still at the table looking again at Penelope's letter to her friend.

Then he put it into his pocket.

With what might well have been called admirable control he proceeded to open the rest of his letters which were of no particular interest.

Then he walked into his study where his secretary was waiting for him. There was quite a pile of letters to be signed and a number of invitations to accept or refuse.

Even though he was seething with rage inside, the Duke talked in his usual quiet way to his secretary who had no idea how angry he was.

"I understand, Your Grace," he started, "that after luncheon, which as you know is taking place in the House of Lords, you will be leaving for Hampton Court."

"Yes, I will be going there for tea, Blackstone," the Duke replied, "but I may not be returning for dinner. I have an appointment I think, but I am not sure."

"You have indeed, Your Grace, you are dining with His Royal Highness this evening but not until nine o'clock as His Royal Highness has a levy, I understand late in the evening."

"Yes, of course, I had forgotten," the Duke replied.

But he knew as he spoke it would be an admirable reason for leaving Penelope as soon as he had made it clear to her that he had no deeper intentions of any sort and certainly not what she expected of him.

When he left his house an hour later he had finished all his correspondence and his carriage was outside.

The meeting that followed the luncheon party took longer than the Duke had expected.

So he was not free until mid-afternoon to drive to Hampton Court.

It was a lovely day and the sun was shining brightly on the River Thames.

He thought if he was as happy as he should be, the sunshine would have entranced him.

As it was, the more he thought about what had occurred and what he had meant to Penelope, the more it made the world seem somehow darkened and distant.

'Why should I ever worry? Why should I care?' he asked himself.

Yet he realised that the kiss he had given Penelope had meant more than any kiss he had given to a woman for a long time.

Of course he had kissed a number of eager women, most of them married.

But he had known, as he did so, that they found him extremely attractive and would, if it had been possible, accept any offer he had made to them.

To them, as they were already married, his title was not significant. They had found him attractive as a man and that was exactly what he wanted.

Now, he told himself, he would make it quite clear to Penelope that he had no intention at all of pursuing her otherwise the sort of letter she had written to his cousin's daughter might be read to a great number of his relatives and friends.

He might, although it did seem unlikely, be forced into offering Penelope marriage, just because she could say that he had damaged her reputation.

As his horses travelled with such speed, he reached the house of Penelope's father much sooner than he had expected.

He turned up the drive and saw the house in front of him and he had a sudden desire to drive away and leave things as they were.

But if he did so, he was quite certain that Penelope would make more trouble than she had already.

It was therefore essential, both to him and to her, that he should straighten things out and the truth should be the truth and not deception.

"I hope not to be too long," he said to his coachman when the horses came to a standstill. "So don't go to the stables, but wait for me. If I am longer than I intend to be, I will let you know."

"Very good, Your Grace," the man answered.

The Duke walked into the house.

The butler showed him into the room overlooking the river that the Duke had been in many times.

There was no one there and for a brief moment the Duke thought that perhaps Penelope was not at home.

Then, even as he queried it to himself, the door opened and she came in.

She was looking very lovely, there was no doubt about that.

Because she was smiling and her eyes were shining as she walked towards him, he thought that the letter she had written to his cousin's daughter could not be true.

He was holding it in his hand and, as she reached him, he said and his voice was hard,

"I have come to see you because I am exceedingly upset by the letter I received this morning."

"That is not the way I would expect you to greet me," Penelope said. "I have been looking forward to seeing you this afternoon."

"I was looking forward to it too," the Duke replied. "But I received this letter which you wrote to my cousin's daughter."

As he spoke, he handed the letter to Penelope.

By the way she stiffened when her eyes fell on it told him all too clearly that she realised she had made a *faux pas*.

"I just cannot understand," she said, "why Charlotte should have sent this letter to you."

"It was her mother who did," he answered, "who, as you know, is my cousin. I brought it to you because I thought that we had both been mistaken over what a happy and joyous occasion the night before last was and made it into something serious."

Penelope stared at him.

"What are you saying?" she asked.

"I am saying that you were '*counting your chickens before they were hatched*'," the Duke replied, "and I think we were both unnecessarily temperamental when we were in the Conservatory."

There was silence and then Penelope said sharply,

"I just don't understand what you are saying to me except that you appeared to be wooing me in one way or another."

"I was kissing you," the Duke replied, "as you have kissed a great number of men and I have kissed a great number of women, I do *not* wish you to make the mistake of taking it more seriously than it was intended."

He paused for a moment before he added,

"We had a most delightful dance and the kiss was nothing more serious than we expressed our delight at the way we had danced together."

Penelope stared at him and there was no mistaking the anger in her eyes.

"Are you trying to say that you have no wish to marry me?" she questioned.

"I have no wish to marry anyone," he answered. "To be truthful I have been pressured by my family over and over again to take a wife. But I do *not* intend to marry until I am older and so the question of an heir must wait."

"And you came here to tell me all this?" she asked angrily.

"I had a distinct impression that you were expecting something different, and as I did not want you to make the mistake of telling people what was untrue and the sooner I came to see you the better."

Penelope walked over to the window.

He thought that she was forcing herself not to rage at him as she really wanted to do.

Instead, after quite a long silence, she said,

"Can you really be so indifferent to what I feel for you?"

"You expressed that very clearly in the letter to my cousin's daughter. Therefore, while I hope, Penelope, we will always be friends, I wish to make it quite clear that there is no question of my marrying you or, for that matter, anyone else."

It was then that Penelope lost her temper.

She turned round to face the Duke and shrieked,

"You are a swine and a cad and I loathe you! How dare you come to me and say such things? How dare you infer that I expected to marry you? I assure you of the number of men who have asked me to become their wife, you are certainly not – at the top of the list!"

Her words appeared to tumble over themselves and the Duke bowed.

"You have made it very clear to me where I stand," he replied. "I can only say, Penelope, that I am delighted to have met you and to have danced with you, but, as that is all, I am completely content."

He then walked towards the door.

"I hope," he said as he reached it, "that you will tell Charlotte that you were mistaken and your affection was not for me but for someone else."

Before she could reply, he left the room closing the door firmly behind him.

Although he heard a loud scream, he did not know if Penelope was cursing him in language which would have shocked her mother and father.

The Duke walked briskly to the front door.

As he climbed into his carriage and a footman was about to close the door, a girl then came running out of the house and to his very considerable surprise jumped into the carriage beside him.

"Take me away! Take me – away!" she begged the Duke. "Please, *please* take me away!"

She flung herself, as she spoke, onto the seat beside the Duke.

He saw that tears were running down her face.

The footman closed the door behind her.

Without realising that there was anyone else in the carriage, the driver of the very fast pair of horses started to move quickly away down the drive.

The Duke was about to say 'stop' when he realised that he recognised the girl's tear-stained face and her fair hair.

She had been at the party the night he had kissed Penelope and he remembered now that she was a relation of some sort.

He therefore did not stop the carriage as he had intended to do, but asked as she sat up on the seat,

"What has happened? What has upset you?"

"He was all I had to love – and he loved me," she stammered in a broken voice, "and now he is – dead."

The tears were rushing down her face and she put both her hands up to her eyes.

The Duke saw from the movement of her shoulders that she was sobbing bitterly.

Because she was small and somehow seemed to be utterly pathetic, the Duke then moved from the back of the carriage onto the seat beside her.

"Now tell me what this is all about," he said gently.

Sobbing she next turned to hide her head against his shoulder and he now realised that her whole body was shaking in her sorrow.

"Now you must not cry like this," he urged her. "You must tell me what has happened to upset you."

"He was all I had," the girl sobbed, "and – she has had him killed. Now I am completely and utterly – alone."

The words seemed to come jerkily between her lips.

Because the carriage was moving and the Duke was sitting next to her, she was still hiding her face against his shoulder.

He was aware of the sweet scent that came from her hair and which reminded him of wild flowers.

As they turned down the drive, he wondered what he should do with this unhappy girl. But he thought that it would somehow be cruel to take her back to where she belonged.

Pulling a large white handkerchief from his pocket, he gave it to her and suggested,

"Now wipe your eyes and, if you can stop crying, you must tell me what I can do to help you."

"No one can – help me, no one!" she moaned. "I only wish I was – dead too."

The words came stuttering from between her lips.

The Duke was wondering again if he should stop the carriage or allow it to keep going.

Now they were out of the drive and on the road and the horses were quickening their pace.

"We are leaving your home," he said. "As you have no possessions with you, I don't know where you are going or if I am able to take you there."

"She killed him! She killed – him!" the girl sobbed, "I don't know how to live – *without* him."

Now the Duke wondered if he should draw up the carriage, turn it round and take her back to the house.

Then he thought that it might be a mistake to stop so near to Penelope's home or to have anyone aware of what was happening.

She was still weeping hysterically on his shoulder.

He thought that never in his life had he experienced anything quite so unusual and at the same time so difficult to cope with.

As they came in sight of Hampton Court Palace, the Duke then had an idea.

He had been there so often with his mother and father that the people in charge of The Palace knew him.

He had often gone into the garden alone while his father was contributing something.

"Stop at The Palace!" he then abruptly ordered the coachman.

A few minutes later they turned in at the gate and the Duke said to the girl who was still crying against his shoulder.

"We will go and walk in the garden of The Palace and you can tell me what your trouble is and I can try to solve it. But I think it would be a mistake for people to see you crying as you are now."

"I am – sorry," the girl murmured and wiped her eyes again with his handkerchief.

As they drove up to the door of The Palace and one of the attendants came hurrying out, the Duke said,

"Good evening. I have a lady with me who wishes to see the garden and I hope you will not mind if I leave my carriage outside for a short time."

"Of course not, Your Grace," the man answered who recognised the Duke. "The garden is looking fine at the moment."

"I feel sure it is," the Duke replied.

He turned and helped the girl, who was holding his handkerchief up to her eyes, out of the carriage.

They walked on into the garden of Hampton Court Palace, which was renowned for its beauty and array of exotic plants from all over the world

The sun was shining benignly on the River Thames.

He thought as they reached a seat near the river that they were unlikely to be disturbed.

In fact there was no one else to be seen anywhere in the garden at this moment.

As he helped the girl to sit down and sat beside her, he began gently,

"Now please tell me what all this is about and what has upset you."

CHAPTER TWO

"I was – upset," she said in a voice he could hardly hear, "because they had – my dog killed."

As she spoke the last word she put the handkerchief that the Duke had given her up to her eyes.

He realised that she was now making every effort to keep herself from sobbing hysterically.

"There is no hurry," he said gently. "We have lots of time. Just tell me first of all why you were staying with Penelope's parents and why your dog was with you."

"He was the only thing I had left, the only thing – I had to love," was the answer that came in jerky tones from behind her hands.

The Duke waited for her to go on and he did not continue the conversation.

After what seemed a long pause, the girl said,

"I am so sorry, terribly sorry – to behave like this. I know men hate to see women crying. But I loved him so much and he was only playing – he was not hurting the swans."

The Duke was finding this difficult to follow.

And after a moment he said,

"You have not told me why you were staying with the Dentons."

With a great effort the girl took the handkerchief from her eyes and replied,

"They were the only relations I could think of who I knew were somewhere near my home."

"So, they are your relations?" the Duke repeated.

It was actually a question and after a moment the girl said,

"My mother was a cousin of Penelope's mother and she had often said it would be nice for Penelope and me to be friends. So when Mama died and I had nowhere else to go, I took Jo-Jo and arrived at Cousin Claud's house."

"Was he surprised to see you?" the Duke asked.

"He was very kind and felt that it would be nice for Penelope to have a friend with her and, of course, as there was nowhere else for me to go, I must stay with them," the girl told him.

The Duke who had always thought of Penelope's father as a decent sort of man could only murmur,

"That at least was kind."

"Yes, it was, but Penelope did not want me. She was angry when her friends, especially – if they were men, talked to me and she was always trying to put me in the background."

The Duke thought that this was not surprising, but he enquired,

"Yet they gave you a home when you did not have one."

"It was a home for me and I thought for Jo-Jo too, but I soon learnt Penelope did not like animals especially dogs and kept saying he had to live in a kennel – outside the house."

She gave a little sob and with an effort continued,

"He had always slept on my bed – always."

Now the tears were back again.

The Duke was silent for a long moment before he quizzed her,

"You must tell me what happened today."

"Two friends of Penelope's had dropped in to ask her to a party and she was telling them then that she was to be engaged to you," the girl replied. "At that moment, as they were standing by the window overlooking the garden, a man shouted out that – Jo-Jo was chasing the swans."

"I suppose that the swans belonged to Penelope's father?" the Duke enquired.

"Yes, and he was very proud of them. But Jo-Jo was just having fun and making them and the little cygnets, which had been born a month ago, plunge into the water," the girl said. "But he would not hurt them. He has never hurt anything – ever since I have had him."

She paused for breath.

The Duke was about to ask her a question when she went on,

"It was then that Penelope shouted, 'Kill him! Stop him! Shoot – him! He must not hurt the swans'."

It was impossible for the girl to continue because she was crying again.

After some minutes had passed the Duke said,

"So they shot your dog?"

"And threw him into – the river," the girl sobbed. "I love him and he had been with me ever since he was born and – now I will never see him again."

Because the torrent of tears were shaking her, the Duke put his arms round her.

"You have to be brave," he said. "It is a terrible thing to have happened, but if he did not suffer he would not want you to be unhappy."

"I am trying – not to cry," she said, "because Papa always said men hated women who cried, but I cannot help it because – I will never see him again."

As she was clearly so upset, the Duke could think of nothing he could do but hold her a little closer.

Then thinking over what she had just said he asked almost sharply,

"Are you really saying that Penelope was telling the visitors that she was engaged to me?"

There was a pause before the girl answered,

"She said that you were going to be engaged, but that they were not to talk about it until it was announced in the newspapers."

The Duke drew in his breath.

He was sensible enough to recognise that if people were talking about his engagement and if she had written to Charlotte and also told some visitors, she was then quite capable of telling a great number of other people.

Under those circumstances her father would indeed be justified in claiming that the Duke had now ruined her reputation and he would be forced to marry her.

For a moment he felt as if he was being seized by giant hands into a position that he could not escape from.

As the girl in his arms wiped her eyes and made another effort at being brave, he said almost as if the words were put into his mouth by unseen hands,

"As you are asking for my help, I am asking for yours and please will you be kind enough to help me?"

What he said obviously surprised the girl.

Moving her head from his shoulder she said,

"How could I possibly help you, Your Grace, when you are being so kind as to help me?"

"What you have just told me," the Duke said, "has made me feel that I am being driven into a position from which it will be impossible to detach myself unless I act very quickly and you help me."

"How can I?" she asked hesitatingly. "I do want to help you because you have been so kind to me. I am sorry to have cried and – ruined your handkerchief, but I did not know what to do. I have lost Jo-Jo for ever and I cannot go back to that horrible and beastly house where – they killed him."

"I can understand your feelings," the Duke replied, "and I want you to understand mine. Because what you have just told me now has made me realise that I am in an almost intolerable position where I will just have to marry Penelope, whatever my real feelings are."

"Why should you have to do that?" the girl asked in astonishment.

She was in fact so surprised at what he said that she moved out of his arms and turned her head to look at him.

The Duke was silent for a moment and then he said,

"Living with Penelope you must be aware that she is determined, as she has been such a success, to marry someone with a major title."

He saw the girl's eyes widen before he went on,

"It does not matter to her what the owner is like. What she wants is to crown herself with an important title which will be a magnificent climax to her success as the most beautiful *debutante* of the Season."

"Yes, but, of course, that is what she wants," the girl agreed. "She said so often to me, 'I will beat them all. I will end the Season with a Wedding which everyone will want to attend and no bride could be lovelier than me'."

"Especially," the Duke then commented, "if she is marrying a Duke."

"Naturally that is what she wants," the girl replied. "That is why she intends to marry you, Your Grace."

"But I have no wish," the Duke retorted, "to marry her. Or anyone else for that matter. That is exactly why I am begging you, almost on my knees, to help me."

The girl looked bewildered.

Now that she had stopped crying, the Duke could see that she was very attractive in her own way.

In fact she was not only, in his opinion, as beautiful as her cousin Penelope, but she also had something in her eyes and her expression which was different.

'It is,' he thought, 'that of intelligence.'

Something that was seldom obvious in the paraded and much talked of *debutantes*, but which strangely enough he could see quite clearly in this young girl's expression.

"You asked me how you could help me," the Duke said, "and I don't want to frighten you, but it is the only way I know of how you can do so."

"Of course, I will help you," the girl replied. "You have been so kind to me in taking me away from – that horrible house where they killed Jo-Jo. I will do anything you ask me to do, but I am afraid that you are going to ask me to find somewhere where I can stay until I can get in touch with – Mama's other relatives."

The words came slowly from her lips and after a pause she added,

"I know that most of them are far away in the North – of England."

"What I am suggesting," the Duke said quietly, "is that you allow me to find you somewhere to stay and more important still allow me to announce that we are engaged to be married."

The girl stared at him as if she had not heard him correctly.

Then he explained quickly,

"Our engagement will only be a pretence one and it will only last until Penelope gives up pursuing me. Then I promise to find you somewhere to live where you will be very happy and with people who will love you and take care of you."

"That is what I want," the girl answered. "But how can you possibly do that for someone you have just met? So how is it possible for us to pretend to be engaged to be married?"

"That is really quite easy," the Duke replied. "We will merely announce our engagement in the newspapers. But we have to do it very quickly before Penelope's father tells me I have ruined her reputation and as a gentleman I must make an honest woman of her."

He spoke sarcastically and only when he saw the question on the girl's face did he add,

"I promise you, you will not be frightened. We will just behave as an ordinary couple who enjoy each other's company until Penelope is looking elsewhere for a titled husband and both you and I will have escaped from her and her family."

The girl stared at him incredulously and then said,

"You make it sound very possible but will everyone really believe that we are engaged when we have only just met?"

"How are they to know?" he asked. "Penelope may be suspicious but if she says so, it will only make people either laugh or be sorry for her because she has been badly treated. It is much more likely that she will merely toss her head in the air and profess that I proposed to her, but she refused me."

"Everyone who knows her will know that is a lie," the girl replied.

"What they say or do not say will not affect us," the Duke said. "We will go to the country and after the first announcement say that we have to wait for the Wedding because we are still in mourning for one of our relations."

He paused before he added,

"That actually is the truth, because I heard only last week that a relation of my father's, who I have not seen for two or three years, has just died in Ireland."

There was silence for a moment.

Then the girl said,

"You are so kind and so understanding and I am ashamed of myself for being what my Mama would have called 'unrestrained.' But I loved Jo-Jo so much and he loved me. No one else loves me and no one wants me."

The way she spoke was so pitiful that without even thinking the Duke put his arm round her and drew her close to him.

"Now you have to be very brave," he said. "One good thing is that Jo-Jo did not suffer. He would have died not only from the gunshot but from being thrown into the water."

He coughed before he went on,

"Try not to think about it and I want you to meet my dogs and I feel sure you will find that one of them will give you some pleasure, even though I know that in your heart you will never forget Jo-Jo."

"Oh, you understand, you really understand!" the girl cried. "And because you have been so kind to me – I want to help you if it is at all possible."

"It is possible," the Duke replied. "We are going to drive back to London now and stop at where I know the newspapers are printed and, then when Penelope wakes up tomorrow morning she will have a shock."

The girl did not miss the note of satisfaction in his voice.

Then, as if he did not wish to linger talking about Penelope, he suggested,

"Now I want you to tell me about yourself. But, as time is getting on, I suggest we go back into the carriage and hurry to London."

The girl wiped her eyes once again and murmured,

"I will do anything you want. But you do realise that I have come away without a thing to wear and without a penny piece."

"Those are unimportant things," the Duke replied. "One step at a time and now we are going to London just as quickly as my horses can carry us there."

He rose from the seat as he spoke and, taking the girl's hand, he pulled her up beside him.

"You have to be brave," he told her again, "very brave and the first thing you have to do is to smile at any of the servants who see us and make them believe that we have enjoyed our visit to Hampton Court Palace."

The way he spoke made the girl laugh.

Although it was little more than a smile, it seemed almost to transform her from someone very miserable into someone young and he had to admit, very attractive as well as very beautiful.

As they got into the carriage having told the guide, who had shown them into the garden, that they were very impressed with it, the Duke took a piece of paper from his pocket and a pencil.

"Now," he began, "you have to answer, as if you were at school, questions that it is necessary for me to have the answers for."

The girl gave a little chuckle and said,

"I hope they will not be too difficult for me to give you the – proper answers."

"They are quite simple I can assure you. First of all, what is your name?"

The girl smiled.

"It does seem strange when you have been so kind to me and we have been so close that you really have no idea – who I am."

"I agree with you," he answered her. "At the same time it is essential that I should get it right."

He hesitated before he went on,

"We were not introduced in the formal fashion, as we should have been, but I can hardly become engaged to someone without a name!"

"Of course not!" she laughed. "My name is Devinia and my other name is Mountford. My mother was a cousin of Penelope's mother."

"And so that is why you went there when you had nowhere else to go," the Duke declared.

"Yes, that was why I went to the cousin my mother had often told me was a very sweet and loving person," Devinia said. "But she could not control Penelope who did exactly what she liked. She was often, I thought, rude to her mother while she was obedient and respectful to her father."

The Duke thought to himself that they all seemed rather unpleasant.

Having written down Devinia's name, he asked,

"Now you must tell me about your father."

"My father was a soldier," Devinia began, "and he was killed nearly six years ago when he was fighting with his Regiment abroad."

She stopped for a moment before she added,

"That is why Mama and I had very little money and lived quietly in the country."

She gave a deep sigh before she went on,

"We were very very happy and I had Jo-Jo to talk to when Mama was busy or visiting friends, who all loved her as I did."

"I can understand that," the Duke said. "So your father was a soldier and what was his Regiment?"

"He was in the Coldstream Guards," she told him. "He was just going to be made a General when he was so sadly killed."

"So you are the daughter of, shall we say, General and Mrs. Mountford and that is how it will appear when our engagement is announced."

Devinia pondered for a moment and then she said,

"I forgot to tell you that Mama had a title of her own, as her father was in the House of Lords. However, he died before I was born and Mama often told me that as he was so clever she wished that I could have met him."

The Duke was thinking that this was even better than he had expected.

He felt that, at least, his engagement would sound very respectable.

None of his family, at any rate, would be critical or think that he was intending to marry someone who was not accepted socially.

It took some time to reach London as the traffic seemed rather heavier than usual.

But eventually the carriage drew up outside a large ugly building where the Duke knew that *The Morning Post* was printed.

Leaving Devinia in the carriage he walked in by the front entrance.

On informing the man at the door who he was, he was led directly to the Editor's office on the first floor.

"This is a great surprise, Your Grace," he said when the Duke was announced. "I never expected you to pay us a visit even though, as you well know, we have written a great deal about you one way and another."

"I have something more important than usual which I want you to print tomorrow morning," the Duke told him. "It is my engagement."

The Editor threw up his hands.

"You are engaged!" he exclaimed. "So those who have been betting, and there are quite a number of them, that you will remain as you always have been, a devout bachelor, will lose their money. Now tell me, Your Grace, who is the fortunate woman to capture your heart and I will be surprised if I don't guess who it is?"

"I shall be extremely surprised if you do guess the lady's name," the Duke replied with a smile. "Therefore I will not embarrass you, but I have written down exactly how I want the announcement to be made and I would be exceedingly grateful if you could put it in every edition of your newspaper tomorrow."

"Your Grace, it will be our top news as the betting against you getting married has been increasing Season by Season and those who are certain that they would select the winner sooner or later have always gone away with their tail between their legs."

The Duke laughed.

"Well, this time they will win their bets, although I will be surprised if they guess correctly."

He put the piece of paper which he had torn from his notebook on which he had written very clearly in his neat handwriting,

"The engagement is announced today between His Grace the Duke of Lavenham and Miss Devinia Mountford.

The bride is the daughter of the General Archibald Mountford, who was killed in action in India six years ago, and Lady Irene, who was the daughter of the sixth Earl of Tiverton."

The Editor read it through slowly.

Then he turned to the Duke and remarked,

"This will most certainly surprise a great number of people. I have not heard of the lady who has won your heart and, although I do remember the death of the General six years ago, I am sure that I am right in thinking that the Marquis of Tiverton died earlier without leaving an heir."

"I expect you are right," the Duke said. "I never worry myself about those sort of things, but leave people to read about them in *Debrett's Peerage*."

The Editor laughed.

"You would most be surprised at how many copies are under the pillows of *debutantes* as soon as they leave school. They all want titles and who could want more than to be a Duchess."

The Duke put on a lofty air as though he was not interested in what the Editor was saying. Even though he knew that it was surely the truth.

"I will be extremely grateful to you," he replied, "if you can print this to appear first thing tomorrow morning."

"Of course, it will be on the front page," the Editor assured him. "But I have to say that what we would really like is a photograph of Your Grace and, of course, your fiancée."

The Duke spread out his hands.

"There, unfortunately, I cannot help you," he said. "My fiancée has been in deep mourning for her mother and has only recently come up from the country."

34

"Then I would hope that you will allow us to take a photograph of you both as soon as possible," he proposed.

"You must make contact with my secretary to make the arrangements," the Duke said in a lofty tone, "for the simple reason that we are leaving for the country almost immediately and it would be therefore impossible for you to photograph us before we leave."

"We will surely try, Your Grace," the Editor said, "and thank you sincerely for giving us the opportunity of beating our opponents at what will tomorrow be the most sensational news for the ambitious Mamas who put a Duke at the very top of the list of eligible bachelors and this will certainly leave a gap!"

The Duke laughed heartily as he was meant to do and walked towards the door.

The Editor hastened to follow him to escort him to the carriage where Devinia was waiting.

He stared at her with the greatest interest and the Duke realised that he was really wondering if he had seen her before.

How was it possible that the Duke was marrying someone who had, as far as he could recall, not appeared in any of the social lists of *debutantes*?

The Duke shook him by the hand and climbed into the carriage.

He was aware as he drove off, that after peering in as hard as he could at Devinia, he was scratching his head as he found it impossible to remember if he had ever heard of her let alone seen her before.

The carriage carried Devinia and the Duke back to his house in Berkeley Square.

It was a very fine mansion which had been in the hands of the Dukes of Lavenham for over two centuries and the Duke was very proud of it.

At the same time he cared more for his ancestral home in the country which again had been handed down century after century.

Every reigning Duke had contributed something to Laven Castle itself.

Few people, however, had the privilege of enjoying the fine collection of pictures and furniture that had come from France and other countries in Europe.

"I have no wish to have strangers clumping about on my valuable carpets," the Duke's father had said, "and prying into places where they are not wanted."

So he had refused to allow visitors unless they were close friends to come to Laven Castle.

The Duke, when he inherited, had been amused at the curiosity that his contemporaries in the Social world gave his home.

He was allowed, as he grew older, to have a few friends to stay with him at The Castle for the Hunt Ball and for the shoots which took place in the autumn.

Otherwise the Duke's family had very much kept themselves to themselves and the public, however curious they might be, remained outside.

He was sure now that if he took Devinia to the country tomorrow as soon as the announcement of their engagement hit the Social world, there would be only a few friends who would be brave enough to follow them to the country.

It would be easy to refuse to open the door to the more curious of the Press.

What the Duke was thinking about as they drove towards Berkeley Square, was that he had taken revenge against Penelope's cruelty.

To make her happy again he must provide Devinia with another dog which she could love as she had loved Jo-Jo.

Just before they reached Berkeley Square, Devinia said again to the Duke,

"I suppose you must realise that I have come away without any clothes and I only have what I stand up in."

The Duke laughed.

"We have not thought of that," he said, "but it need not worry us, I will tell you why. My housekeeper, who has been with me for a number of years has, I know, a collection of dresses that go back down the centuries and she will, I am quite certain, find you something which may be a little old-fashioned, but will surely be very becoming."

He thought he heard a sigh of relief from Devinia and went on,

"In the country my housekeeper there has an attic full of past relics including delightful dresses worn by my mother and my grandmother that I have always been told are just so beautifully made that the wearer does not feel embarrassed as they have not come from Bond Street."

He chuckled as he added,

"It makes them appear as enchanting and as elegant as if they had just stepped down from one of the pictures."

"That is very reassuring," Devinia said, "because I am feeling equally embarrassed at having to tell you that I have no money with me and, I am afraid very very little in the Bank."

She paused before she went on,

"Mama was ill for a long time before she died and I had to pay doctors and nurses and, of course, the servants, which left me with practically nothing when I went to my cousin for help."

"Don't worry about any of those things," the Duke said airily. "I promise you the housekeepers will delight in finding someone who needs their attention and if you look as I said as if you had just stepped out of a picture, who could expect anything else in a house in London which is very old and much older when you reach the country."

"Are we going there?" Devinia asked eagerly. "I do love the country and, of course, I need not tell you that I love riding."

"There are stables filled with so many horses which are extremely annoyed that I have not been exercising them as I ought to do," the Duke replied.

Devinia laughed.

"You make it a joke, Your Grace, but to me it is like stepping into a Fairy story. I feel that at any moment I will wake up and find that it is all a dream."

"That is what it is," the Duke said. "A dream and you just have to forget what has happened recently and tell yourself that you are stepping back in the past and the past for you was very happy and full of interest."

"You are so kind," Devinia said, "and it is difficult for me to say how grateful I am. At the same time you do realise that Penelope will be very angry and I am sure in some way she will try to avenge herself on you and me."

The Duke laughed.

"Let her try!" he exclaimed. "Most women are so ineffective that they could not even begin a battle against an enemy. Even if we are in this, as far as Penelope is concerned, we have a considerable fortress both here and in the country to protect us and what is more important the goodwill of those who are genuinely fond of us."

He felt that he was really thinking about himself as Devinia had made it perfectly clear that she had very few relations and practically no friends except the dog which she had really loved.

'I must make it up to her in some way,' the Duke thought. 'I am sure that there will be a puppy of some sort waiting for us in the country and it is essential we should go there as soon as possible.'

He was not so stupid as to not appreciate that his engagement would astound those who had heard him say so often that he had no wish to marry.

But it would utterly and completely confound those who had been sure, if he did choose a wife, it would be Penelope because she was so beautiful and becoming so successful in the Social world.

In fact no one would have been the least surprised if after all she had captured the elusive Duke.

'A bachelor is what I have been and that is what I mean to remain,' the Duke told himself firmly.

He knew that he had made it very clear to Penelope and her father that he could not be forced into marriage, which he was quite certain that they intended to do.

It was an old story and a great number of men had been forced to put the ring on a woman's finger because they had, to most intents and purposes, ruined her social reputation and he must therefore pay the price by making her his wife.

There was a story whispered around London that an ambitious mother had even gone so far as to ask the Prince of Wales to make it clear to one of his friends that he had to marry the girl who he had, at a dance, spent a long time with in the garden instead of being seen on the dance floor.

And the young Marquis of Worcester had to marry a girl after he had been seen talking to her for nearly two hours in a Conservatory.

As Devinia was taken upstairs to her bedroom by a servant, the Duke went into a sitting room.

He thought that he had been cleverer than many of his friends and associates had been in the past.

'I will never marry,' he told himself, 'until I fall in love and marry someone who loves me as a man and not because I am a Duke.'

He told himself that, as this was almost impossible, he would be most fortunate beyond words if things worked out exactly as he wanted them to do.

'Perhaps it is too much to ask?' he questioned.

At the same time in announcing his engagement to Devinia he knew that he had put a barrier between himself and Penelope that would be difficult for anyone to remove.

With Devinia, he told himself, things would be very different.

She was penniless and she was without a father or a mother and now, having played the part he had asked her to do, when things were clear and there was no chance of him being forced up the aisle with Penelope, he could find Devinia someone who would look after her and befriend her and reward her with enough money to be comfortable with in the future.

Eventually she could be married to someone who loved animals as she did and settle in the country where no one in the Social world would hear of her again.

'It is working out perfectly,' the Duke told himself. 'But in the future I am going to be more careful than I have been in the past. When I marry, in perhaps eight or nine years' time because I need an heir, it will be very different from being pushed into a marriage by a greedy, ambitious young woman like Penelope who will never love anyone except herself.'

He drew in a deep breath.

As he turned from the window to see a footman bring him a glass of champagne, he thought as he raised it to his lips that he would drink a toast to himself and his own cleverness.

CHAPTER THREE

The Duke was driving his own phaeton with four horses that he had recently bought which were perfectly matched.

Beside him was Devinia who, because she was so thrilled with the horses, had forgotten for the moment her own problems and looked smiling and happy.

Behind them came a large carriage loaded with the Duke's luggage and the few things that the housekeeper in London had put in a case for Devinia.

"You'll find that Mrs. Shepherd in the country has everythin' you require, miss," she said, "and I've just put in the things that you'll find you'll need immediately you arrive like underclothes and, of course, nightgowns."

"You are very kind," Devinia said, "and I am more grateful than I can possibly say."

When she came downstairs, the Duke urged her,

"Hurry up, the sun is shining and the sooner we are out of London the better. I know you will enjoy the drive."

When she saw that he was driving his phaeton, she was thrilled.

"I have always wanted to ride in one of these smart phaetons," she said, "but it has never come my way. I am so thrilled with your beautiful horses, they are so perfectly matched."

"They are very proud of it," the Duke answered, "and so am I. Now I want to show you how fast they can go. In fact the driver of the carriage is already muttering that he does not think he can keep up with us!"

Devinia laughed.

"That means he loses face with his fellow workers and you will have to give him a start so that he does not lag behind us too much."

"I will give him one while we have luncheon," the Duke said. "He will either go hungry or gobble it down quickly."

She laughed again.

"Most people would rather be slow and late," she remarked.

"If there is one thing I dislike," the Duke retorted, "it is women who keep you waiting for a long time. But I can see you are ready in time to leave and that is what I hoped you would be."

Devinia smiled.

He felt that when she was smiling and not crying she really looked very lovely.

But he had plenty of other matters to think about at the moment.

There were some last minute urgent orders for his secretary, which included instructions that no one was to be told exactly where they had gone.

Then he picked up the newspaper which had been put out for him at breakfast and carried it with him to the phaeton.

He was quite certain that all over London when the elite of Society opened their newspapers, they would gasp with astonishment when they saw the Duke's engagement to a young woman they had never heard of and never seen.

How was it possible that he had found someone he wanted to marry and none of them had been aware of it?

He could almost hear their voices chattering to each other in amazement.

Equally he knew that Penelope would be absolutely furious.

'Serve her right!' he thought to himself. 'She has obviously treated this poor child very badly and at least she will have a home for the time being. Then I will find her a nice husband so that she never need be troubled by those dreadful relations again.'

He understood only too well the shock it had given her in having her beloved dog killed and then thrown into the river.

It was the sort of thing, he thought, that no decent person would do to any animal, let alone one who was as loved as this one had been by a young girl who had for the moment no one else to love and depend on.

When they reached the phaeton, Devinia ran from one horse to another commenting on their beauty.

"How clever of you to find them!" she exclaimed. "You must be proud to own such unusual and marvellous horses."

"Who are waiting to carry you to The Castle," he answered. "So get in and see how fast they can travel."

Devinia was now wearing a pretty straw hat that the housekeeper had given her. She also had a woollen cloak to put over her shoulders if she felt cold.

This she set down beside her because the sun was shining and she thought if anything, although the phaeton was open, she would feel too hot.

The Duke put his top hat on at a rakish angle and he was exceedingly well-dressed and was, she felt, almost too smart for someone like herself.

'I am lucky, very very lucky, that he is so kind to me,' she thought. 'I am sure it was Mama who sent him to save me because if he had not been there I think I should have followed Jo-Jo into the river and drowned myself.'

Then she thought whatever happened she must not be hysterical as it would only annoy the Duke.

She forced herself to speak quietly to the horses and then ask His Grace just how far it was to his house in the country.

"It will take us about an hour after we have finished luncheon at what is an excellent Posting inn," he replied, "which is the very best on this particular road."

Because she had learnt that men, when they were driving, did not want too much conversation, Devinia sat down comfortably on the seat beside the Duke.

She thought that this was something she had never expected would happen to her.

Her father and mother had only been able to keep three horses in their stables that had originally been built for many more.

But they were fine animals and Devinia had loved riding them whenever she had the chance.

She remembered now that her father had often said what outstanding horses the Duke of Lavenham owned.

When he had won a race, her mother was always delighted that a relation was keeping up with the family reputation of being outstanding when it came to horseflesh.

'I never imagined I would get to know the Duke,' Devinia thought as she sat there beside him. 'I am sure that Mama is as pleased as I am with him now.'

She had known from the moment she entered her cousin's house that she was not welcome.

While Penelope disliked her and was aggressive the moment she appeared, her parents thought her to be rather a nuisance.

They complained audibly when they had to spend any money on her behalf.

'Now that I am running away from them,' Devinia mused, 'and so thank you, thank you, Mama, wherever you are for looking after me and helping me as you are now.'

It was a prayer she felt went straight up to the sky.

She must have turned her head upwards because the Duke said unexpectedly,

"Are you looking for clouds or are you expecting to see an angel peering down at you?"

"I think that an angel has already done so," Devinia answered, "because he or she has sent you, Your Grace, and I never, never thought I would be so lucky as to ride behind your marvellous horses who are far faster than I could ever have expected."

"That is what I like to hear," the Duke answered. "I will look forward to showing you the other horses I own, two of them have won very large races and I have several others I have high hopes for in the future."

"Do tell me about them?" Devinia enthused. "Did you choose them yourself or were they brought to you as they knew that you would want to buy them?"

This was the sort of conversation the Duke usually had with a man.

But he then answered Devinia's questions and was surprised when she asked him details about the horses he had never expected from a young girl.

They reached the Posting inn which was two and a half hours out from London.

Although it was early for luncheon, the Duke said, because he was in a hurry to reach home, they would eat while they had the chance.

Devinia enjoyed the food which was exceptionally good.

She thanked the publican in a way which delighted him and which the Duke thought was very tactful.

When they climbed back into the phaeton, it was to find that the carriage had indeed gone on ahead of them.

In fact it was nearly three quarters of an hour since they had left, the ostler of the inn told them.

The Duke chuckled.

"I do know," he said, "that my Head Coachman dislikes having to lag behind and he is now making every effort to reach home before I do."

"I should have thought your Head Coachman, Your Grace, and you were far too old to behave like boys who always want to beat each other at every game!"

"Perhaps we never grew up," the Duke responded. "Horses, I am convinced, make most men ambitious and that every horse which does well is a credit to its owner."

Devinia smiled.

"I am sure that is true and so you will understand, when you are kind enough to mount me on a really fine horse, I will do my best to beat you!"

"In which case," the Duke said, "I will give you a very slow donkey!"

Devinia gave a cry.

"I had one once when I was very small. I remember trying to race a very tiresome boy, who lived near us, who had a pony about the same size, but unfortunately it was faster than my donkey!"

The Duke laughed.

"There you are! We go through life doing the same things over and over again and find each time it is more exciting than it was the last time."

"I did not find it at all exciting on my donkey when I was always left behind," Devinia protested. "Then, when

I could ride Papa's horses, he always kept the fast one for himself."

There was silence for a moment and then she said,

"But he was killed when I was quite young and then Mama and I found it very difficult to keep anything except one horse which drew a carriage for her."

There was a rather sad note in her voice which the Duke found very touching.

"I will give you a very fast horse to ride," he then promised, "and you may beat everyone on it, but not me!"

Devinia grinned.

"I will try," she replied.

"Then I will do my very best to prevent you from humiliating me," the Duke answered.

"I would never do that, Your Grace. Whenever she had the chance Penelope always humiliated me in front of her other guests. I felt shy and embarrassed, but there was nothing I could do about it."

The Duke reflected that the more he heard about Penelope the less he liked her.

He was prepared to thank God on his knees for having saved him from a wife who was everything that he most distrusted and disliked.

It was his mother who had said to him when he was very small,

"You have to remember, my darling, that people are very easily hurt by those who have while they have not. Therefore, because you are such a very lucky boy and have much to be thankful for, you have to be kind to everyone else and never ever make them feel that they have been humiliated because you have more than them."

He had not understood what she had meant at first.

Then, as he grew older, he realised that the ordinary people would almost expect a Duke to treat them as if they were of no standing and to assert himself as their superior with almost every word he spoke.

He had, therefore, always remembered to praise the people who served him and, when they were friends, never to boast about the things he possessed which were better than theirs.

*

When two hours later they turned in at the huge gates which led to the Duke's house, Devinia gave a little cry of delight.

"These are just the sort of gates you ought to have for a big and famous house," she said. "I love the touch of gold on them and, of course, the two cottages on either side where it looks as if they have stepped a Fairytale book."

The Duke smiled.

"Wait until you see the house," he replied. "I have always felt that it might have come straight from a Fairy story rather than being, as it is, a Castle which was built in Queen Elizabeth's reign and added to by every member of my family ever since."

Devinia was gazing with delight at the huge oak trees on either side of the drive.

Then she saw the ancient bridge which led the way over the stream that flowed in front of the house.

She gave a cry of approval.

"I thought that you would have a stream near your house," she said, "and I did not dare ask if you have a lake in case you said 'no' and I would have been disappointed."

"I am hoping that you will not be disappointed at anything you find," the Duke replied. "I have loved every inch of my home ever since I was born and so you cannot praise it too much as far as I am concerned."

"Of course I will praise it because it is polite and I would hate you to be disappointed with my views. But now I can do it with joy and excitement simply because as far as I can see you have everything I have ever wanted to see in a big ancestral house."

She was looking as she spoke at the Tower, which was at one end of the building.

Even as she did so the Duke's standard was run up the flagpole on the roof to show that the owner was now in residence.

It unfurled in the wind and Devinia clapped her hands.

"It is lovely, lovely!" she cried. "No one could have a better Castle to reign over than you, Your Grace."

"Thank you," the Duke answered. "Most people start by being envious and then by being critical. I am so delighted that you are so enthusiastic at first sight. I only hope it is something you will not lose when you come closer to the house and then walk inside it."

"It is a Fairy Castle and nothing you can say or do will change it," Devinia said. "I think your ancestors must have done everything they had to do with love. That is what I feel that The Castle is, it is a Castle of Love to make the world a more beautiful and kindly place because it is here."

The Duke thought of all the people who he had entertained at The Castle and the praise he had listened to, it had never been quite so charming as how Devinia had just put it.

"That is what I want you to feel," he said aloud, "and welcome to your new home."

She gave him a quick glance.

He knew she was thinking it might not last long and he would soon find some excuse for getting rid of her.

He did not understand why but he could suddenly read her thoughts.

Yet there was something in her eyes as well which told him without words what she was thinking.

He drew up the phaeton outside the front door.

Instantly two grooms came running from the side of The Castle to go to the horses' heads and hold them still.

"Afternoon, Your Grace," one of them said. "Did Your Grace 'ave a good journey?"

"A very good one and I believe that I must have broken all records," the Duke answered.

"Well, the carriage arrived just ten minutes ago," the groom informed him, "and they was real pleased to find they'd beaten Your Grace."

"I think they must have cheated by eating little or no luncheon," the Duke replied laughingly.

Then he helped Devinia out of the phaeton.

Holding her by the hand he took her in through the front door.

There was a grey-haired butler waiting to welcome them and three footmen in smart livery.

Devinia thought that they looked as if they were just going on the stage.

She was thrilled and enchanted by everything that she saw in The Castle.

When the Duke ushered her into the drawing room which his mother had furnished with Louis XIV furniture and some exquisite French china, she gave a cry of delight.

"You must be so proud of this room," she enthused, "it is so lovely! The furniture and china must be the envy of everyone who comes here."

"My mother was particularly proud of this room," the Duke replied, "and now I must show you my father's favourite."

He took Devinia down a long passage which was hung with ancient tapestries with beautiful inlaid furniture along the walls.

As he opened a door at the end of it, he commented,

"I have a feeling that you will really be impressed, Devinia, because this is our library."

Devinia gave a gasp.

The library was very large and beautifully planned, and the books with their bright colours were on shelves that went right up to the ceiling.

It was, without any exception, the most impressive display of books that Devinia had ever seen anywhere.

"It is lovely, lovely!" she exclaimed, "and I want to read every one of them."

The Duke laughed.

"You would be at least one hundred and fifty before you managed it!"

"In which case I had better start reading at once, Your Grace."

"No!" he answered firmly, "I still have more rooms to show you including the Picture Gallery and what must not be forgotten, The Castle's ballroom."

"Do you often give a ball?" Devinia enquired.

"Not always my own. I loan it to the local Hunt when they have their Hunt Ball. It is also used at Election time when speakers come down from London and are very impressed at being given such a good background."

"I am not surprised," Devinia said. "I should think they would be ashamed if they don't win after impressing the people who listen to them with their eloquence as well as a platform which would, they would expect, carry them straight into the House of Commons."

"That is what they all hope it will do," the Duke agreed. "But sometimes they are disappointed."

He took her to the back of The Castle where there was a beautiful flower garden as well as two very old and fine fountains throwing water up in the air towards the sky.

When the water caught the sunshine, it was almost blinding and it fell into an exquisitely carved bowl beneath it.

"It is absolutely beautiful," Devinia said. "How can you own anything as lovely as all this and leave it for one moment? I should be so frightened it might vanish and I would come back to find it was all a dream."

"I come back and think I must go on dreaming," the Duke answered. "I always hope when I reach home that I have left all my troubles and difficulties outside the gates."

"I am sure that you do and nothing could make you happier than to be here in your Castle of Love," Devinia burst out spontaneously.

He next introduced Devinia to Mrs. Shepherd, the housekeeper, who was told that she had no clothes except for the few things that had been packed for her in London.

"Now don't you worry about that," Mrs. Shepherd said, who was rustling in her black dress. "As I've often said to His Grace, I've enough clothes here to stock a shop or to dress the Queen herself and what I wants is to see it on someone pretty like this young lady."

"That is a compliment," the Duke said. "I suggest, Mrs. Shepherd, we take her upstairs and put her in one of the most comfortable rooms and see if, after all you have said, you have enough clothes to dress her so that she looks entrancing."

"You leave it to me, Your Grace," Mrs. Shepherd replied.

There was a note in her voice which told all too clearly how thrilled she was at this opportunity.

A little later when she was told that tea was ready, Devinia walked into the drawing room to find that there was a special cake which had obviously been hastily made as soon as the morning newspapers had arrived.

On it was written in large letters,

"*All happiness to you both on your engagement and every blessing for the future.*"

"We will have to go to the kitchen after that, Your Grace," Devinia said after she had looked at it, "and thank the cook. Has she been with you for long?"

"Years. She came when my father came into the title and she has been longing for me to get married and frightened that she might die before I do so."

As he finished speaking it flashed through his mind and he knew that Devinia was thinking the same thing that when their engagement was broken off the staff would feel in some way that they had been to blame.

Devinia said nothing.

'It was funny,' she thought, 'that he could read her thoughts.'

Then he said in a very quiet voice,

"What we both have to do is to live for today and not anticipate what might happen tomorrow."

"I should so like to think," Devinia answered, "that there were no clouds in the sky. But you know as well as I do this is only a way to save you from Penelope and quite frankly I am afraid of what she might do."

"You are not to think of such things," the Duke told her firmly. "She can do nothing but accept the situation as it is. I am afraid that you will also have to put up with the members of my family who will, of course, be immensely curious as they have never heard of you before."

He paused before he added,

"But they will be delighted that I am preparing to marry when I have been so positive in the past that I would not be hurried and would wait for many years before I even thought of taking a wife."

There was a harsh note in his voice as he spoke.

And the smile went from Devinia's lips.

Then she said very quietly,

"As you and I both know, this is only a game. But it will easily become something rather more frightening if we keep anticipating what might happen in the future."

The Duke did not speak and she went on,

"We are both pretending to be well-off and so it is essential that people should not guess that we are acting a part. So we must try to enjoy our subterfuge as much as we can. I for one am more thrilled than I have ever been at seeing your lovely Castle and thinking I have just stepped into a dream and I have no wish to wake up for a long, long time."

The Duke laughed.

"You are absolutely right. Now after what you have been through you should have a rest before dinner. I am quite certain the cook and those who assist her are planning something really fantastic for our first night in The Castle."

Devinia gave a cry of joy.

"That will be exciting and something I shall look forward to."

"Well go up now and have a rest," the Duke told her. "And I hope I will have something to show you when you come down to dinner which will be intriguing for you as well as a surprise."

"Now you are making me feel curious, Your Grace, and instead of resting I will be wondering what it will be."

"No guessing," he affirmed, "or no surprise!"

"That is unkind," Devinia replied. "But before I go down on my knees and ask you to tell me your secret I will go upstairs and talk to the housekeeper. I am very curious to see what clothes she has for me."

She did not wait for the Duke to answer but slipped out of the room.

He thought inwardly that everything was going far better than he thought it would.

He was wondering not only what his family would say when they read the newspapers, but just how Penelope would react.

Even the thought of her made him scowl.

Because he had no wish to remember the danger he had been in, he went out to the stables.

He was greeted by his Head Groom who was full of what a success he had had with the horses.

The Duke let him talk for a time and then he said,

"By the way, Plumb, the young lady I am engaged to has just lost her dog which she loved very much. Have you, by any chance, or do you know anyone who has a dog or a puppy which requires a new owner?"

"Now it's funny you should ask that, Your Grace," Plumb said, "as Albert the gardener's got a new puppy that were born just last week. Its mother had to be put to sleep after it were born."

He hesitated before he went on,

"The vet said there was nothin' they could do for it. You can imagine, Your Grace, that Albert were real upset after havin' her for so long."

"I am sure he was," the Duke replied. "But we can easily find him another guard dog, which I now remember that his dog was."

"We've thought all about that already, Your Grace, and we've heard of a very fine dog that its owner wants to sell as he has too many of 'em."

"Then, of course, we must buy it," the Duke said. "In the meantime what about the puppy?"

"It's givin' Albert a lot of extra work, as he has to hand-feed it and as Albert said he's too old and too busy to spend so much time with it."

The Duke did not wait to hear anymore.

He went straightaway off to Albert's house and his wife showed him the puppy which was a small attractive spaniel who was, she claimed, always hungry.

"Well, I have someone who will be very delighted to feed him," the Duke told her. "May I take him back with me now?"

"Of course, Your Grace, and to tell the truth I be glad to be rid of him. My husband's had to feed him night and day and there be so much goin' on in the garden. As it happens, he'll be feedin' himself very soon."

"That is all the better," the Duke replied.

Carrying the puppy and saying that he would send a footman back for his food and the basket he slept in, he walked back to The Castle.

The butler told him that Miss Mountford was still upstairs with the housekeeper.

Carrying the puppy in his arms, the Duke went up the stairs and, knowing which room she was in, he knocked on the door.

"Come in!" he heard Devinia call out happily.

As he entered the room, she was wearing what was an extremely attractive dress and admiring herself in one of the long mirrors.

"Oh, it is you, Your Grace!" she exclaimed.

Then, as she saw what was in the Duke's arms, she gave a cry.

"A puppy!"

"His mother is dead and he is looking for someone to love him," the Duke said putting the dog into her arms.

"Oh, he is just so sweet! Absolutely sweet! And of course I do love him already. Can I really have him for myself?"

"He is all for you," the Duke answered. "I am told he is very hungry and requires food constantly, although he might be able to eat on his own in two or three days."

"I will feed him, I will look after him and I will love him," Devinia promised. "Thank you, thank you, you could not have given me anything I want more. Although no one will really take Jo-Jo's place, this one will certainly come second."

The Duke smiled at her.

He thought that if he had given a woman a diamond necklace costing thousands of pounds she could not look more pleased than Devinia was.

She was holding the dog close to her and talking to him just as human beings should talk to animals.

The Duke realised she had, for a moment, forgotten everything else, the clothes she had been so thrilled with and himself as well.

She was just giving her heart to the small puppy she was holding in her arms.

"Is it really *for me*?" she asked after a moment.

"It is yours completely," the Duke replied. "All you have to do is to look after him and love him."

"Of course, I will," she promised at once. "What is his name?"

"As far as I know he has not been named yet and so you can christen him."

"Of course, I will," Devinia replied. "I will think of a marvellous name for him because I feel sure he is going to be, when he grows up, a very fine and handsome dog."

"That is up to you, Devinia," the Duke reflected.

He was just about to say something more when he realised that Devinia was not listening to him.

She was talking to the puppy in a way which made him aware that she cared for him already and now he was snuggling against her.

The Duke looked at his housekeeper and smiled,

"I see I am not wanted. I expect even your lovely dress will now take second place."

"She'll look real beautiful in them all, Your Grace," Mrs. Shepherd remarked.

"I am quite sure she will with your help," the Duke replied.

He walked from the room and down the passage to his own bedroom.

As he did so he was thinking again that fortune was on his side.

In saving himself from Penelope he had found by accident the one person who would play the part with great success and without any complaints.

'Things might well have been so different,' he told himself as he walked into his own room.

It was now difficult for Devinia to think about the dresses when the Duke had given her this lovely puppy that needed all her attention, her care and, of course, her love.

However, as he had fallen asleep in her arms, she put him down on the end of the bed.

When she saw the frown on the housekeeper's face, she said,

"I promise you he will not make a mess. I am sure I will be able to find him a basket where he will sleep and, of course, he will need a bowl for his food."

She had hardly finished speaking when there was a knock on the door.

A footman came in carrying the two items she had mentioned which had been collected from the little dog's previous home.

He was fast asleep but just murmured a little when Devinia put him into the basket.

Then she put the food she was to feed him with in a bowl and some water from her wash-stand into another.

"I realise that you are worried," she said to Mrs. Shepherd, "but I have looked after a dog who I have loved dearly ever since he was born. And he was always clean and our housemaid at home said he was the best behaved dog she had ever seen."

"Well, I hopes this one's the same," Mrs. Shepherd replied a little tartly.

"I promise you he will be," Devinia assured her, "and please help me with these dresses. I don't want His Grace to be ashamed of me when his relatives come to look me over. Also I would expect, his neighbours."

"I am afraid, miss, you will find they will all come here. They have always been that curious about His Grace that I've sometimes felt like tellin' them to mind their own business."

Devinia was listening wide-eyed as she went on,

"As they often says to me, 'who's takin' his fancy now and is he engaged to anyone yet'?"

She paused before she added,

"Of course, I could not be rude to any of them as they were friends of His Grace. But I felt like tellin' them that no man whoever he might be wants people pryin' into his private affairs and pushin' their daughters at him hopin' they will end up with a Duke in the family and thinkin' how much kudos it'll give them."

"I can understand in a way that it is because a Duke sounds so romantic that they would want to have him in their family," Devinia said. "But no one has any right to ask questions that concern only the person they are talking about or the woman they hope he will marry."

"That's quite right, miss," the housekeeper replied, "and what I thinks myself. My mother always used to say, '*curiosity killed the cat*' and I've often thought them who was curious about His Grace should have a sharp lesson. But then who's to stop them bein' curious about anyone as handsome and as charmin' as His Grace."

"I am sure you are all very fond of him," Devinia said.

"We are, indeed, miss. We only hopes you'll make him happy. Between ourselves I never thought he'd marry so soon. He always swore he'd wait until he were older and then settle down with a wife and family."

Devinia felt that she should say nothing to this.

So she only replied,

"Of course you want him to be happy and I will do my best."

"That's what I hopes you'd say," the housekeeper said smiling. "Now, I've ordered your bath and you'll have a real pretty gown to please His Grace at dinner. I'll try to get some jewellery from the safe to go with it."

"It sounds very very exciting," Devinia said, "and thank you for being so understanding."

Mrs. Shepherd then left the room.

Devinia ran at once to look at the puppy and he was fast asleep in his basket.

She thought that he was very beautiful although she was not quite certain of his breed, but felt that he must be a spaniel.

"I will look after you," she told him in a soft voice. "I am sure I will grow to love you as I want you to love me. We are very lucky, you and I, to be here with someone as kind and generous as the Duke."

She gave a deep sigh as she went on talking to the puppy.

"I did not know, when I was so unhappy yesterday, that anyone could be as kind as the Duke is being to me. Now on top of everything else he has given you to me."

Then she lifted her eyes up to the sunshine coming in through the window.

Not in words but in her heart, she now said,

'Thank you, Mama, for sending him to me. I know for the moment I am safe and I am no longer utterly and completely alone as I was when I lost Jo-Jo. Please, please, Mama, do *not* let this wonderful dream end too quickly.'

CHAPTER FOUR

Mrs. Shepherd found an exceptionally pretty dress for Devinia.

It had a wide and almost crinoline size skirt and a tight bodice ornamented with the most beautiful lace.

"I thought it was exactly what you needed for your first night in The Castle," Mrs. Shepherd said. "It must have belonged to the Duchess who was painted by all the great painters at the time as the most beautiful woman in England."

Devinia smiled and replied,

"In which case I had better wear a yashmak over my face so that they only look at the dress!"

The housekeeper smiled too.

"I thought you'd have an answer, miss, But it be a long time since we've had anyone as pretty as you in The Castle."

Devinia thought that this must be an exaggeration, as the Duke would have had his friends here as Penelope had often talked about all the ladies who had fallen under his charm.

Although, Devinia had gathered, they were mostly married ladies.

She remembered her mother saying once that a man who did not intend to be rushed up the aisle with some ambitious *debutante* invariably spent his time with married women who could not ask the same of him.

She kept trying to think of things that her mother had said to her so as to interest the Duke.

And to make sure that he did not send her away too soon from The Castle simply because he found her boring.

'Maybe the pretend engagement will indeed last for months,' she told herself hopefully.

At the same time she had the distinct suspicion that once Penelope realised that she could no longer have him, she would marry one of the other men who had already asked her, but who were not as prestigious socially as the Duke.

'It is so wonderful here,' she thought to herself as she finished dressing. 'I want to stay and explore not only the house but everything around it.'

She was about to ask the housekeeper if she should go downstairs when there came a knock on the door.

She turned round to see the Duke.

"Can I come in, Devinia?"

"Yes, of course, Your Grace," she replied.

"I felt that you should come now and meet your chaperone who, I may have already told you, is my great-aunt who has been ill for a long time."

Devinia did not speak and he went on,

"She never leaves her bedroom and I was going to take you to meet her in the morning as she is usually asleep at this hour. But the nurse has told me that she is awake now and longing to meet you."

"Then I will come as soon as I am ready," Devinia answered, "and can I bring my dog downstairs? I thought I would take him out into the garden before or after dinner."

The Duke ruminated for a moment and then said,

"I think it would be a mistake to take him with you to see my great-aunt at the moment. But I know that Mrs.

Shepherd will arrange for him to be taken downstairs and he will be there when we have seen her."

Devinia smiled at him.

"I thought you would arrange everything perfectly," she said. "I promise not to be a bore with my dog."

"Why should you be?" the Duke enquired.

"My cousin Claud said I was a bore, a nuisance and a great many other things which I will not repeat," Devinia said quietly, "just because I wanted Jo-Jo to be with me."

"As far as I am concerned, you can have your new dog with you day and night," the Duke told her. "But I do think you should give him a name."

Devinia looked at him enquiringly and he went on,

"I believe you have thought of a name already."

"I have, as it happens, but now that I have to say it aloud I think perhaps you will think it silly."

By this time they were walking down the passage together and there was no one to overhear them.

Then the Duke asked her,

"Well, go on, tell me the name."

"Because he is so charming and I think he will be amazingly handsome when he grows up, I want to call him 'Prince'," Devinia replied. "Or would you think that is a mistake."

She looked at him anxiously and the Duke laughed.

"In other words your dog would be socially more significant than me and, of course, you are quite right. It will put me in my place and I will not feel as you think I am feeling, so uppish that girls like your cousin will do anything to join me at the altar."

Now the hardness was back in his voice.

As they moved down the passage, Devinia put her hand on his arm.

"Please don't let what has happened spoil you," she said. "Mama always said when things went wrong we were to pray that the sun would shine tomorrow and we would forget very quickly that we had been hurt or that people had been unkind."

"Your mother was so right," he agreed. "You and I will make a vow here and now that we will not think of the past or keep referring to why we have had to come here."

He paused before he carried on,

"We will just enjoy ourselves hour by hour and day by day until all that is wrong and unpleasant fades into the past and we forget about it."

Devinia clapped her hands and gave a jump of joy.

"That is just what I wanted you to say!" she cried. "This house is beautiful and everything in it is so perfect, I could not bear you and I to spoil it by talking about the things that have made us unhappy."

She thought to herself as she spoke that she must not mourn Jo-Jo and once again the Duke had shown his kindness to her by producing another dog for her.

By this time they had reached the end of the long passage and at a door just ahead of them a nurse appeared.

"Good evening, Your Grace," she said when she saw the Duke.

"Good evening, Nurse," he replied. "How is your patient today?"

"I am glad to say her Ladyship has had a quiet day and has slept for most of it. It would be a mistake for you to stay long as I want her to be kept quiet. But she is very anxious, as you can imagine, to meet your fiancée."

She looked at Devinia as she spoke, who held out her hand.

"It is very nice to meet you," she said, "and if I can help you in any way while I am here, I will be very pleased to do so."

The nurse smiled at her.

"That is very kind of you, ma'am, and I will take you at your word. I think sometimes it is good for my patient to talk to people she does not see every day."

The nurse did not wait for an answer but pushed open the door behind her.

It was a very large and very lovely bedroom.

There was a huge four-poster bed on which lay the Duke's great-aunt.

She had been a beauty when she was younger and she still was an attractive woman despite her grey hair and the lines under her eyes.

The Duke moved forward and bent to kiss her.

"Good evening, Aunt Helen," he said. "I am so glad you are awake and I can introduce you to my fiancée. As I expect you have already been told, her name is Devinia."

Slowly the old lady held out her hand.

Devinia took it in hers and bent to kiss it saying,

"I am so glad you are well enough to meet me."

"As my eyes are so bad," the old lady said, "I find it difficult to see you. But I am sure if Ivan has chosen you for his wife you are very beautiful."

Devinia laughed and then she responded,

"I want him to think so and he has told me that you were acclaimed a great beauty when you were my age."

The Duke had not said so, but Devinia knew that it would please the old lady.

"That is true. I remember men just like Ivan telling me that I was as beautiful as the spring. They all wanted to take me up to the moon."

She spoke slowly finding difficulty in remembering her words.

Devinia thought that they were very touching and then she said,

"I promise you I will try to make him happy. I am sure that is what you want me to say."

"Of course, it is. Keep him close to you and don't let him run away. Today I hear too often of women losing their husbands and you must never do that."

"No, of course not," Devinia agreed.

The old lady closed her eyes and the nurse said in a quiet voice,

"I think she is tired and you should leave her now."

It seemed strange to Devinia but almost as she said the last words, the old lady had closed her eyes and almost fallen asleep and was now breathing quite gently.

The Duke took Devinia by the hand and drew her towards the door and as he reached it he said very quietly,

"Thank you, Nurse. Let me know when I can come again."

"Of course, Your Grace," the nurse replied and they left the room.

Devinia felt that it was one of the really strangest conversations that she had ever had.

But she thought that it was typically part of The Castle and something she would always remember.

They walked down the stairs without speaking and only when they reached the dining room did the Duke say,

"You were splendid. Most people are embarrassed by my great-aunt as she only has a few minutes when she is aware of what is happening around her and then nearly always falls asleep if she is listening to someone."

"I think she is wonderful," Devinia replied quietly. "And exactly who one would expect to find in a Castle like this."

The Duke laughed.

"You are making it all into a Fairytale again and are not believing it is real."

"I am so afraid it is not real and I will soon wake up," Devinia admitted.

He laughed again.

"I will not allow you to do that. Not until you have ridden some of my best horses which they tell me are badly in need of more exercise."

Devinia's eyes lit up.

"Can we ride tomorrow morning?" she asked.

The Duke nodded.

"As early as you like and I usually try to reach the stables at eight o'clock."

"Then I will do the same," Devinia replied. "Your very kind housekeeper told me that she has found a riding habit which will fit me like a glove."

"Could anyone ask for more?" the Duke asked.

"You are very kind," Devinia murmured. "I keep thinking I will wake up and find this is all a dream and I am lying in the horrid little room they gave me when I was staying with my cousin Claud. "It overlooked the yard and there were plenty of rooms which looked over the river but they were too good for someone like me."

The Duke frowned.

It always annoyed him when he heard about people being badly treated or what, in his opinion, was being 'set down' in case they thought they were good enough to have the best. They were therefore given the worst so that they should not get 'uppish' in any way.

It was what he had encountered in his life because, when he was the heir to a Dukedom, the boys at school teased him in case he should feel swanky.

There were certain friends of his father and mother who, because they were jealous, went out of their way to take him down a peg or two.

They talked of all sorts of things while they were having dinner in the gracious but imperious dining room. In particular places overseas that the Duke had visited and Devinia had read about in her books.

"I long to go to China," she said, "and I would love to see the Pyramids of Egypt. But I have had to imagine them by reading about them in books. I just hope that one day I will be lucky enough to see them in reality."

It was with difficulty as she spoke so wistfully that the Duke did not say that he would take her to both places.

But he told himself he should not raise her hopes just in case their pretend engagement came to an end and there was no chance of her going abroad.

The nearest she would get to the Pyramids or to China would be to read about them in books.

"What I would like," Devinia was saying, "while I am here, which might not be for very long, is for you to tell me about the places you have visited and what they meant to you. I have always wanted to discuss what I have read in books with someone who has actually been there. But I saw very little of my father because he was a soldier and, when he was at home, my mother wanted to spend every minute she could with him."

"So you were left outside," the Duke remarked, "and it is something I have often been myself so I know exactly how you felt."

Devinia did not reply and he went on,

"I had never been abroad and it was not until I had taken my father's place that I was able to travel as I had always wanted to do."

"Oh, please do tell me about your travels," Devinia pleaded. "I want to know exactly what you felt when you first visited Greece and, if when you did so, did you feel that the Gods were still there?"

There was silence and just for a minute she thought that the Duke was going to change the subject or perhaps to disillusion her about Greece.

Instead he said,

"I had, of course, read about the Gods on Olympus and the Shining Cliffs of Delphi. Like you. I wondered if it was just invented by the writers and perhaps the Gods themselves had never really existed."

Devinia drew in her breath.

"But you were sure they had," she said almost in a whisper.

"I felt a very strange feeling when I first reached Greece," the Duke admitted, "which increased as I moved round from place to place. It was almost as if the Gods themselves were directing me and telling me that they were real. Although many centuries have passed by, they are still there if we look for them."

Devinia gave a deep sigh and clasped her hands in her lap.

"You felt it! You were sure of it!" she said. "It is what I feel myself, so please, please do tell me more about Greece because it has always meant so much to me. There has been no one who ever wanted to discuss it with me."

It was almost, the Duke thought later, as if she had hypnotised him into talking in a way that he never done before to anyone.

He told her of his feelings from the very moment he stepped ashore until he finally left Greece.

Because it meant so much to him he knew that the feelings that the Gods and Goddesses had evoked within him would remain with him all through his life.

The Duke talked to Devinia in such detail as he had never talked before to anyone.

When they eventually left the dining room and the candles were burning low, they were both feeling as if they had visited the stars.

"Now you must go to bed," the Duke urged. "We both have to be up early and we have done a great deal today and I hope have left a great deal behind us as well."

"I hope so too and thank you, thank you," Devinia replied. "I will go to bed and dream I am in Greece and I can only tell you that it is almost as wonderful to me as it must have been to you."

She did not wait to say anything more but ran up the stairs.

She only stopped at the last step to look down and to wave her hand because he was still standing in the hall.

'She is most certainly very unlike any other woman I have ever met,' the Duke mused to himself, as he walked towards the study.

In her bedroom Devinia wanted to dance with joy that she had had such a fascinating evening.

She knew it was something that she would always remember while the evenings that she had spent with her cousins Claude and Penelope she wanted to forget.

'I can only hope,' she thought before she said her prayers, 'that the Duke will not be free from Penelope too quickly and therefore I will have to stay and protect him.'

She undressed and knelt for her prayers before she climbed into bed.

She thanked God profusely for looking after her and for bringing her here to The Castle.

It was only by a stroke of luck and by Penelope's appalling behaviour in telling those people secretly of their engagement that had prevented the Duke from proposing to her that he might so easily have done.

Perhaps it had been God or perhaps his mother who had saved him from a girl who was only interested in his title and would doubtless have then made him exceedingly unhappy if they had married.

Penelope would never have understood if she had listened to what he was telling her tonight about Greece.

She had said once that she did not believe in all that nonsense, as she called it, about Heaven and people caring for one after they were dead.

"When you are dead, you are dead!" Penelope had said. "So I intend to stay alive and be myself and no one else until I am very very old."

She had always resented the fact that her father had insisted that they all went to Church on Sundays.

"Who wants to sing those silly hymns?" Penelope had questioned. "If I pray I pray not to God to make me beautiful but to Papa to give me enough money to make myself as outstanding and as lovely as everyone expects me to be."

She had seen that Devinia was listening to her and she continued,

"You mark my words! If you want things you have to fight to get them for yourself. There is no angel in Heaven to pop down to earth to give it all to you."

Devinia had not argued with her because she knew that it would only make Penelope angry.

She would never agree to anything that she had not thought of herself.

'If nothing else,' she now reflected, 'I have saved the Duke, just as he saved me, from being unhappy for the rest of his life.'

She looked a little wistful as she said aloud,

"If only I could have saved Jo-Jo too, it would be the most wonderful thing that had ever happened!"

Then she told herself that now she had Prince and only a man as kind as the Duke would have found another dog for her so quickly and one that was so adorable.

"Thank You, thank You God!" she said again as she climbed into bed.

She was quite certain that her mother, who was in Heaven with Him, was smiling down at her.

Because it had been a long and tiring day as well as an exciting one, Devinia fell asleep at once.

*

She woke when the housemaid came to call her, as she had asked her to do, at seven o'clock.

She pulled back the curtains and, as the sun came streaming into the room, Devinia jumped out of her bed and ran into the bathroom.

She had been careful to ask that her riding habit should be laid out for her the night before.

It was only half past seven when she was dressed and now ready to go to the stables and the maid who had helped her into her riding clothes said,

"They fits you like a glove, miss. If you asks me, you'll look ever so smart on His Grace's fine horses."

"Thank you," Devinia smiled. "I only hope I will not fall off! I have not been able to ride for nearly a year."

She had asked her step-uncle, almost as soon as she had arrived, if it was possible for her to ride. And he had told her quite firmly 'no'!

"I hire horses for myself," he had told her. "But Penelope does not ride. I therefore see no reason for you to need that amount of exercise when you will doubtless be dancing almost every night."

Devinia did not argue with him, but she had missed riding more than she could possibly say.

When there were horses in the stables, she would pat them and talk to them and long to be in the saddle above them.

Now that she was to ride again, she only hoped that the Duke would think her a good rider, as her father and mother had always thought her to be.

She had just reached the stables when the Duke appeared and he was surprised that she was there so early.

"I believe you are here to try to take my best horse before I am on him myself" he teased her.

"I have been looking at your horses and I think they are all wonderful," Devinia replied. "Please give me one which is almost as fast as yours, as I want to race just as fast as the horses can carry us."

The Duke laughed.

"You must be careful not to fall off," he warned. "Most women I know are content in trotting slowly down Rotten Row so that the men there will admire them."

"The birds and the bees can do that here," Devinia suggested, "and I am sure they are very critical!"

The Duke smiled.

"I have ordered you a horse," he told her, "and here it comes."

It came into the stable yard as he spoke and Devinia saw that it was an almost all white stallion.

It was not only very well-bred but, she was certain, a horse that could gallop very fast if he wished to.

'It is almost impossible,' the Duke thought as she ran towards the stallion, 'for anyone to look as excited and enraptured.'

She patted the animal and talked to him as the Duke remembered his father had always told him to talk to any horse that he was about to ride.

'She is certainly unusual,' he thought to himself.

But, as she was obviously anxious to be off, he said nothing.

He merely mounted the horse that he had ordered for himself, which was one of his favourites.

They went first to the paddock and the Duke said,

"I think that you had better feel your way by taking Pegasus round the paddock before we go into the rougher areas which are on the other side of the stream."

Devinia did not reply, but gave Pegasus his head.

She cleared the jumps that were scattered over the paddock without any difficulty.

Watching her, he told himself that she rode well and so he need have no qualms about racing her.

He had known many women who had talked about how much they enjoyed riding only to find that they had no wish to do anything but trot.

The whole idea of racing was something that was definitely only for men.

Because he was curious as to why she could ride so well, the Duke then took her from the paddock into the land beyond the stream where he had ridden so often.

He had, in fact, never been accompanied there by a woman. But on many occasions with his male friends who had wanted to race him and knew that it was only possible by being as good a rider as he was himself.

He was therefore surprised when Devinia put her horse into a gallop as soon as they reached the open fields.

His own horse had to strain every nerve to keep up with her.

By the time they had drawn their horses to a full stop the Duke was well aware that this strange girl, who had sobbed so miserably in his arms and who had rescued him from her cousin, was undoubtedly a good rider.

One who would be greatly praised and commended whenever she appeared on a horse.

Devinia then drew in Pegasus near to the end of the ground where there was a tall wood where the Duke had often shot.

When he came up beside her, he asked,

"Who taught you to ride like that?"

"My father did originally, but after he was killed I had three of his horses and, as I could not bear to part with any of them, I had to exercise them myself."

She sighed.

"You see we were very poor and could not afford more than one man to rub them down and clean out the stables, but he was far too old to ride at any speed however much the horses needed it."

"Now I see why you wished to be in the country."

"Nowhere I have ever been has been as marvellous as this," she said. "If you let me ride your horses, I only hope I will live to one hundred before you turn me away."

The Duke laughed.

"I promise not to, because I can see how useful you are. I was afraid that Pegasus would be too large for you, but I am sure that he has never had a finer rider on his back as he has had this morning."

"Thank you! Devinia replied. "That is just the sort of compliment I really appreciate, Your Grace."

Then her voice dropped as she added,

"I thought when I went to live with my step-uncle I would never have a compliment again."

"So he would not let you ride his horses?"

Devinia shook her head.

"No, he disapproved of women being fast riders. But I think actually that it was an excuse for not having to provide me with a horse, especially as Penelope only had one which she used in Rotten Row and had no wish to ride at any other time."

"Now I have seen how well you ride," the Duke said, "my horses, ma'am, are at your disposal."

"You could not give me anything else that I would appreciate more," she replied excitedly. "Thank you, thank you and it is wonderful for me to be able to race you."

"We will have one more race before we take the horses back," the Duke suggested. "I think we must both be prepared today for visitors."

"Visitors?" Devinia asked in surprise.

"My loyal friends will want to congratulate me on what appeared in the newspapers yesterday and I would not be surprised if some of my relatives, as well as my friends, came down from London."

He gave a wry smile before he concluded,

"Their curiosity will be more important than their feelings about making the long journey."

The way he spoke made Devinia laugh.

"Now you are frightening me," she said. "I am so terrified of saying the wrong thing."

"All that you have to do is to keep telling them how much you admire me and how happy you are at meeting them and let them make the rest of the conversation."

Devinia laughed.

"It is not as easy as you think. As I have no wish to tell lies, they are certain to ask me how we met and where we met and how was it possible for you to fall in love with someone so unimportant as me and am I looking forward to being a Duchess?"

The way she spoke with her words almost falling over each other, made the Duke laugh.

"I am certain," he said, "you will have a reasonable answer to every one of their questions. At the same time be prepared. You will undoubtedly be asked them and it would be very wise for us to give the same answer to each question."

"Yes, of course," Devinia replied. "I did not think of that problem. Where did we meet? Or shall we think of somewhere better than my cousin's house?"

"I think where possible we must tell the truth," the Duke observed.

There was silence for a moment and then Devinia said in a rather embarrassed voice,

"We can say correctly that you came to the house to see Penelope and not me."

"I went, if I recall rightly, because Penelope asked me," the Duke replied. "It was there that I met you and remembered we had met several years before when I was shooting in the North of England, where I believe you told me you had some relatives."

"Yes, of course, how clever of you to remember! There are several distant cousins of mine in the far North of Northumberland and I remember that my mother had relatives staying at the time and we were asked to a dinner party where you were present."

The Duke stared at her.

"Good Heavens!" he exclaimed. "That was almost six years ago and if I am honest I just cannot remember meeting you."

"I was not important enough or old enough at the time to be introduced to you," Devinia replied. "I merely thought, when I went out with the shoot, that you shot very well. But to be honest I never expected to see you again."

She paused before she said a little shyly,

"Of course I can now say that I hoped and prayed we would meet again if I ever came to London."

The Duke laughed.

"You make everything into a Fairytale and that one will do. I remembered admiring you when I saw you with the people at the shoot and then I had not forgotten how pretty you were."

"We must not make the story of our first meeting sound unreal," Devinia replied. "I think if I remember you, that is as it should be."

"Nonsense!" he exclaimed. "You are very pretty now and you must have been exceedingly pretty at fourteen or fifteen or whatever age you were. And I found that no other woman in London was as beautiful as you."

"No one is going to believe that," Devinia answered firmly. "As you have many people talking about you and what they call your 'love affairs', they are certain to realise that you are not pining for me."

The Duke shrugged his shoulders.

"We do have to give them something to think about and also convince them that I prefer you to your cousin Penelope. Because she was so outstanding and so pretty, she expected to marry a Duke, although, of course, she would doubtless have accepted the Prince of Wales if he had not been already married!"

"Now that is going too far," she protested. "You will spoil it if you make the stories sound unconvincing."

"I am only teasing," he laughed. "I promise that I will behave nicely, but you must not forget how grateful I am to you for saving me."

"As you have saved me," Devinia replied. "I was so happy last night in the lovely bedroom I have in The Castle and the first thing I did when I woke up was to jump out of bed and see if Prince was there or if he was also part of a dream."

"And was he there?" the Duke enquired.

"Of course. He was very good and did not wake me up all night."

"Well, I am sure our visitors will be too curious to be able to talk about anything except why it is possible for me to find a wife who is someone they do not know and have never heard of."

The Duke paused before he went on,

"That is the story and that is exactly why they will be asking you a thousand questions and being immensely puzzled as to why I would prefer you to all the other young women in London who have tried to catch me."

"I suppose there were so many. But you must be modest and not let people realise that you were well aware that they were after your title and not you."

"Now you are being insulting," the Duke protested jokingly. "A lot of women have assured me over and over again that they love me to distraction and it had nothing to do with my position in the Social world."

He spoke with laughter in his eyes and a sarcastic note in his voice which told Devinia that he was joking.

"I think we are safest," she said, "when I play the part which I do extremely well because, of course, it is the truth, that I am only an innocent little country girl and am astonished by the wonder, the beauty and the importance of London."

She stopped for a moment and then, taking up her reins, she added,

"And so, of course, have captured the most elusive Nobleman of all time!"

She was mocking the Duke and, even as he turned to tell her that she must be more respectful, she touched her horse with the whip and Pegasus sprang away.

It was only by really exerting himself that the Duke managed to catch up with her just as the field came to an end and they then trotted into the orchard.

As he drew level with her and before he could say anything she said,

"Please don't be angry with me. It has been such a glorious day and I will always remember it. You must just believe I am playing a part."

She pulled at her reins before she added,

"I am not myself. Not what you would expect of a rather stupid young woman, but what they would expect of someone clever enough to catch and bind you as, of course, at the moment, I intend to do."

She did not wait for the Duke to answer, but hurried across the orchard towards the stables.

He was still laughing when he caught up with her.

When they had taken the horses to the stables and then walked back to the house, it was the butler who met them at the door.

"I think, Your Grace, you'll be surprised," he said, "that no less than three messengers have been here from London to inform Your Grace that members of your family and friends will be arriving for luncheon today."

The Duke sighed,

"I did not expect them to arrive so quickly."

"The messengers were informed yesterday that they were to be here as early as possible," the butler said, "and one of them left at four o'clock this morning."

"Well, they are certainly persistent, Travers, and I am sure we can feed them well if nothing else."

"I'll tell cook, Your Grace, but I think you'll find we'll have twenty extra for luncheon."

He paused then he added,

"Unless others turn up unexpectedly!"

Because she was feeling nervous, Devinia followed the Duke into the hall.

"Who is coming?" she asked when they reached the empty study. "Who can it be?"

The Duke held out both his arms.

"I have not the slightest idea, but I have a suspicion one or two of them will be coming entirely out of curiosity. So be prepared and whatever happens they must not guess for one single moment that we are playing a game."

"No, of course not!" Devinia agreed. "But I have thought of one thing this morning when I was dressing that I think you have forgotten."

"What is that?" the Duke asked.

"Well, I suppose that if our engagement is to look genuine, I should be wearing a ring."

The Duke threw up his hands.

"Of course, you should. How could I have been so stupid? Well, as I showed you before, there are at least half a dozen of them in the safe, so you can have your pick as to which one you prefer. I will get them right away."

"No," Devinia said. "You know if this is real you would go out and choose an engagement ring for me. Then I would exclaim with surprise at how beautiful it is."

The Duke chuckled.

"You are quite right. If we are playing a part, we must play it correctly.

He disappeared at once.

Devinia went to the window and looked out at the garden and for once she was not looking at the flowers.

She was thinking that if this was real it would be thrilling to have a wonderful ring given to her from the superb antique collection which belonged to the Duke.

She remembered them shining when she looked at them, most especially the opal necklace. But he must not give her an opal ring as that would be unlucky.

She was still at the window when he came back.

"I have chosen the prettiest ring of them all," he announced. "It is over two hundred years old and I am sure you will like it."

He took her hand as he spoke and put it onto her engagement finger.

The ring itself was lovely, but it was a little too big and she knew that she could easily have it altered.

The Duke had chosen a diamond ring and in the centre was a large diamond surrounded by smaller ones all of them cut to shine like the sunshine outside.

"It's lovely!" Devinia exclaimed. "Thank you and I will wear it until we say 'goodbye' and then I will be sorry to part with it."

The Duke grinned.

"By that time you might be sorry to part with a lot of things, but for the moment everyone will be impressed by your engagement ring and it certainly becomes you."

Devinia looked down at it and thought that it was the prettiest ring she had seen.

She just wondered if she would be able to wear any of the other jewellery in the special safe, but perhaps that was asking too much.

"I will go and change," Devinia said. "But I think before the visitors arrive we must make quite certain that there are no mistakes in our performance."

"Now you are frightening *me*," the Duke replied. "So, the less we say of substance the better."

"I have chosen the best part," Devinia said as she went to the door. "I will be far too shy to say anything and you therefore can do all the talking, Your Grace!"

She left the room before he could answer her.

But he was laughing as he walked to his writing-table where the messages from London would be waiting for him.

CHAPTER FIVE

It transpired that the Duke, if anything, had under-estimated the interest that his engagement would create.

His relatives, some of whom he had not seen for years, turned up to congratulate him.

Others wrote him long letters that he had to answer as to why, where and who he had found to marry.

After having written out one, he copied the others as they were exactly the same, although he hoped that they would not compare them.

As he had anticipated quite a number of those who called themselves his greatest friends arrived from London to congratulate him, but really because they were intrigued.

Devinia, with the deft help of Mrs. Shepherd, was wearing a most alluring and extremely pretty dress.

She also arranged her hair so that she wore flowers of the same colour as her dress.

It appeared almost as a halo against her golden hair.

"You look lovely," Mrs. Shepherd told her, "there'll be no question as to why His Grace wants to marry you."

Devinia hoped fervently that this was true.

When she went down to luncheon, she realised that a great number of the Duke's friends were astounded by her appearance.

The men fell over themselves in their efforts to pay her effusive compliments. While the ladies present were no less enthusiastic.

After luncheon a number of people who had come from London drove back in their carriages.

There were half a dozen who had arrived late for tea and therefore had to be invited for dinner.

"I am not going to ask you to stay the night," the Duke told them, "because there is a full moon tonight and so you will be able to find your way back home without the slightest difficulty."

"We had not thought of staying," one of them said. "We have only brought what we stand up in and I don't suppose you want to provide all the bedclothes we would need if we stayed the night."

"I have a feeling that more people will be arriving from London tomorrow," the Duke said, "and I have to think of my staff."

One of his friends laughed.

"I feel sure that they are enjoying every moment of it. After all The Castle has been as dull as a grave for years when your mother was ill and again when your father was busy with his affairs in London."

He chuckled as he added,

"There is nothing that servants dislike more than an empty house and a cook always complains if there is no one to praise her food."

"I am sure you are right," the Duke agreed. "My cook is thrilled at being able to cook the food that you have enjoyed tonight. She is already thinking about what she will put in the Wedding cake."

"Oh, when is the Wedding to take place?" one of his relatives asked.

"We have not decided yet," the Duke answered, "because so many of Devinia's friends and relations live in the far North. They would be very hurt if they were not given time to consider how they could come South and you can imagine it requires a great deal of arranging."

They laughed as the Duke spoke sarcastically.

The Duke knew that he was being clever in keeping them from being over-curious as to when the Wedding would take place.

'I am so lucky,' Devinia told herself when she was eventually alone. 'How could I possibly have come from the misery I endured with Penelope to the laughter, fun and comfort of this marvellous place?'

When the third day, after they had received many visitors, had passed and those of them who had come early in the day left before tea the Duke said,

"Enough is enough! If we have any more I shall lock the gates and say 'not at home' to anyone who comes as far as the front door."

"You cannot do that," Devinia argued. "They come because they love you and admire you and I think it is very touching that they are so concerned with your happiness."

"I suppose you are right," the Duke agreed after thinking it over. "At the same time we have done our best to cure their curiosity, which is actually why they are here, and now they can talk about your beauty and how fortunate I am from Rotten Row to the Houses of Parliament!"

Devinia laughed.

"It is really very serious," she said, "as they are all going to be just as inquisitive when our engagement comes to an end and we tell them that we have decided not to be married after all."

The Duke then looked over his shoulder just in case someone was listening and then he said,

"Hush! Even the walls have ears and it is a great mistake for you to say now there is the slightest chance of us being anything but happily married. As the majority of our friends have already pointed out, one must have at least six or seven sons to make quite certain that the Dukedom does not end and be lost for ever."

Devinia looked concerned for a moment.

"It is not a thing to be laughed at. Of course you must have an heir to the Dukedom before you die. But you have plenty of time to think about it and perhaps, when you least expect it, you will fall head over heels in love."

"That is something I wish to avoid at the moment," the Duke replied, "simply because your cousin, Penelope, has shown how easy it is to be defrauded and betrayed by someone one has a real affection for."

He paused before he went on,

"Fortunately I have found out just how crooked she was, otherwise I cannot bear to think what my life with her might have been in the future."

"Forget it!" Devinia exclaimed. "You are free and the whole world is spread out in front of you and if you are bored with London there are a great number of places in the world which you would enjoy and find fascinating as your ancestors must have felt when they brought home to The Castle so many treasures from many different lands."

The Duke smiled.

"Of course you are right and what happens to them could happen to me. As I have a very comfortable yacht, I think it will be expected that we will use it."

There was silence for a moment and then she said,

"I think it would be a mistake for you and I to go abroad without being properly chaperoned. You know as well as I do that would be a bore because we would have to think before we spoke."

Again there was silence.

"She, like everyone else," Devinia continued, "must know that we are playing a part and not, as they believe, really in love with each other."

Before the Duke could speak she added,

"I am perfectly content at present with your horses, and I love being here. So please, please don't be in a hurry for us to set off somewhere else, which as you well know might cause a great deal of gossip that will not particularly be to our advantage."

"The trouble with you," the Duke answered, "is that you are too sensible. At your age you should be leaping with joy at the idea of visiting China or Japan. But I have to admit that you are right and I am wrong and we must stay here until the excitement dies down."

Devinia nodded.

"It will do and they will soon have someone else to talk about in a few weeks or perhaps a month. Then we can make plans."

She gave a sigh before she said,

"But for the moment, let me live in this entrancing Fairy story that I am enjoying so very much."

The Duke laughed.

"You make everything seem real," he replied. "I am quite certain that not a single person of those we have just entertained is not completely convinced we are not madly in love with each other."

"I am sure you are right," Devinia agreed. "But we must be so careful not to let anyone guess the truth or be suspicious that we are acting a part however well."

"I promise not to play the villain," the Duke said. "You must warn me if the halo round my head becomes a little rusty."

"You are too clever for that and now as everyone has gone I think we will be able to have dinner alone and you can tell me more about your travels in the Far East."

"Are you quite certain that I am not boring you?" the Duke asked.

"How could I be bored with anyone so fascinating and so exciting?" Devinia questioned. "If you are tired of telling me your own stories, I would just love to hear about some of your ancestors especially those who brought into the family all the wonderful jewels your housekeeper was showing me tonight."

The Duke smiled.

"I thought the rows of pearls you had round your neck were familiar."

"And the diamonds round my wrist," she added. "I have never felt so grand and you must be very proud to own such magnificent treasures as those which have been collected in this Castle."

"Of course, I am proud of them," the Duke replied. "That is why I would not offend them by having as a wife someone who did not understand or appreciate the way that this Castle has been built up generation after generation."

Devinia gave a cry of delight.

"That is why you have so much to tell me," she said, "and thank goodness there is no one else to listen to us this afternoon."

She greatly enjoyed the excellent dinner which she and the Duke had alone.

They talked comfortably in the Duke's study until it was almost midnight.

Then Devinia, who had listened attentively to every word he had been telling her, went up to her bedroom.

Her eyes were shining like stars as she had been so intrigued by hearing from the Duke his journeys to parts of the world that she had only read about.

"Thank you!" she sighed as she said 'goodnight' to him. "I know I shall fall asleep feeling I am in Hong Kong or some other amazing part of the world. It will be quite a shock to find tomorrow morning that I am back in dear old England!"

"Which you love as much as I do," the Duke said, "despite the fact that you are so thrilled by hearing about foreign lands."

"That was chapter one," she replied as she reached the door. "I look forward to having chapter two and chapter three tomorrow night, and so on as long as we are alone."

She did not give the Duke chance to say anymore, but she heard him laugh as she ran down the passage.

'At least,' she thought to herself, 'he is not bored even though other men might well find one girl like myself rather dull when he could have a party like he had last night and the night before.'

As she reached her bedroom, she was hoping, until it became almost a prayer, that the Duke would continue to enjoy telling her about his travels.

There had not been a moment, which she rather dreaded, when he might believe that being alone with her was boring and then he would have an urge to go back to London where there were, to her knowledge, at least half a dozen beautiful women holding out their arms to him.

'He is just so handsome, besides being so kind and understanding,' she told herself again and again.

She put Prince into his basket at the end of her bed.

She guessed, however, and she was quite right, that he would soon jump onto her bed to be beside her and so continue to sleep there all through the night.

'He is so sweet,' she told herself, 'and I love him so much already. But not as much as I loved Jo-Jo.'

She gave a sigh as she could not think of the dog she had loved for so long without tears coming to her eyes.

Then she told herself that she was being selfish.

As the Duke had been so kind as to give her another dog, she must love him as much as she had loved Jo-Jo and not dwell on the past.

After she had said her prayers, she slipped into bed.

As Prince moved nearer to her, she patted him and told him that he was a good and lovely dog.

Then, because it was after midnight, she closed her eyes and was soon fast asleep.

The Duke also went to bed.

He thought that he had enjoyed the evening a great deal and tomorrow morning he would be riding the new horse which had only arrived that afternoon.

He had slipped away from his visitors to view it.

But he knew that he could not appreciate it as much as he ought to do until he had ridden it.

It had been bought at Tattersalls and he had known its owner before he died.

He had heard a great deal about this particular horse from his other friends who had admired it tremendously. It had been rather expensive, but the Duke was sure that it was money well spent.

And he would confirm it tomorrow morning by the satisfaction he would feel when he knew it would equal, if not surpass, the best of his other horses.

*

He had been asleep for two hours when he woke to hear someone pulling back the curtains in his room.

At the same time calling out,

"Wake up, Your Grace! Wake up!"

He opened his eyes and saw, to his astonishment that the moonlight was still coming through his windows.

His valet, Andrews, was shouting out his name and pulling back the curtains.

"What is it?   What's the matter?" the Duke asked.

"It's what's happenin' below, Your Grace! I thinks someone's kidnapped Miss Mountford!"

"What are you talking about?" the Duke demanded.

He jumped from the bed and ran to the window and he was aware as he did so that there was a dog howling as if in pain below.

"They've gone, Your Grace," Andrews went on, "and they've taken Miss Mountford with them."

"What can you be talking about?" the Duke asked again. "And why is that dog howling?"

"I wasn't asleep," Andrews said, "because I had a bit of toothache. Then I suddenly hears a dog whinin' and then barkin' as if he were hurt. I thought at first it were none of my business. Then rememberin' just what Miss Mountford feels about dogs, I thought it be sure to wake her and she would do somethin' about it – "

He paused for breath and the Duke said impatiently, "Go on!"

"I went to the window, Your Grace, which as you know is above yours. I sees in the moonlight a man holdin' a dog in his arms and punchin' it until it screamed."

"Who was he?" the Duke asked sharply.

"I don't know, Your Grace, but he be a foreigner. Even though it were only in the moonlight, I could see he was not a white man."

The Duke stared at him.

"Are you sure?"

"Quite sure, Your Grace. Just then I thinks Miss Mountford must have heard the dog because she came out in her dressin' gown and went towards it."

The Duke was listening and he could now see the dog which he did not recognise as being one of his.

It seemed, although it was difficult to see clearly in the moonlight, that it was a rather rough common sort of dog which might be seen in any poor street.

"What happened when Miss Mountford appeared?" he asked as the valet had stopped speaking.

"I don't know how to tell you, Your Grace, and I'm sure you'll find it hard to believe."

"Believe what?"

"Well, two men who must have been hidin' by the door, steps forward and throws several blankets over Miss Mountford's head, takes her up in their arms and carries her away."

The Duke stared at him.

"What are you saying, Andrews?" he asked. "Are you telling me the truth?"

"Of course I'm tellin' you the truth, Your Grace! I know it's hard to believe, but that's what they did. I could see them for a moment strugglin' to get the blankets over her head."

He coughed before he went on,

"Then as soon as she was covered they disappears with her round the side of The Castle to where, I suppose they had a carriage waitin'."

The Duke put his hand up to his forehead.

"I cannot believe this has happened!" he exclaimed. "What about the man holding the dog?"

"He puts the dog down still whinin' from what he had done to him and runs after the other men. That was all I saw of them, then I comes up here to tell you what's happened."

"I will now see for myself," the Duke replied.

He put on his dressing gown, slipped his feet into his slippers and ran across the room.

He pulled open the door, ran along the passage then down the stairs to the front door.

The door was open and he supposed that was the way that Devinia had left the house.

There was no one to be seen outside.

If it had not been for the dog lying on the ground and moaning in pain, the Duke would have thought that his valet had been imagining it or suffering from a nightmare.

A glance at the courtyard told him that, if there had been a carriage waiting, it was no longer there.

As Andrews joined him, he quizzed him,

"Are you quite certain that the men who carried off Miss Mountford were foreigners?"

"They were all dark-skinned from what I could see of them. From their clothes I would have thought them to be natives."

The Duke drew in his breath.

Then, as though he was being helped, he found his brain telling him what he wanted to know.

Someone, and it was not hard to think of who that person was, had wanted to get rid of Devinia.

There was only one person who would know better than anyone else that, if she heard a dog suffering in pain or anguish, she would run to its assistance.

That she had been kidnapped and carried away by some foreigner might have been just the imagination of his valet, but the dog was still groaning and moaning from the way it had been treated.

As he could now see clearly that it was not a dog belonging to him or, as far as he knew, to anyone on the estate.

Because he had been trained to use his brain and to make a decision quickly as a soldier would have done, the Duke ordered sharply,

"Tell them in the stables I want my phaeton and the chestnut team to be ready as quickly as possible!"

Before Andrews could answer, he added,

"Then come back here and help me dress and tell the butler I have instructions to give him before I leave."

He was gone before Andrews could reply.

The Duke had learned to dress quickly when he had been at College and he was just putting on his waistcoat when the valet returned.

"They're bringin' the phaeton round as soon as it's ready, Your Grace," he said a little breathlessly, "and do you want me to come with you?"

"No, but have you woken Travers?"

"Yes, Your Grace, and so he'll be downstairs when you are ready."

"I am ready now," the Duke said. "Bring me my shoes and tell my secretary that I will let him know where I will be after I reach London."

He did not wait for an answer, he put on his shoes and ran towards the door.

He left Andrews wondering what he ought to have said before the Duke reached the top of the stairs.

Travers in his dressing gown was in the hall.

"You sent for me, Your Grace," he said looking surprised at his appearance.

"I am leaving for London now," the Duke told him. "Send a man to Dover at daylight to tell the Captain in charge of my yacht that I expect to come aboard tomorrow early in the afternoon and we want to move out of Port at once."

Travers stared at him as he walked to the door.

"See to that dog," he ordered, "and, if he is badly injured, send for the vet."

Before he could reply the Duke turned.

Instead of going out through the front door as they thought he would, he went down the passage to the door to the safe.

No one spoke but Travers smiled.

Both he and Andrews thought that the Duke was picking up a revolver to take with him.

In point of fact when he reached the safes the Duke passed the one which was filled with weapons as well as the one which contained his ancestral silver.

He went to the one which contained all the jewels from which he had recently taken the engagement ring for Devinia.

When he opened the safe door, he saw as she had the first time she had been there, the flashing light coming from the opals.

He hesitated for a moment and then he pulled out the large opal necklace and placed it in his pocket.

He closed the door and just a few minutes later was hurrying towards the stables.

As he expected when he got there the four perfectly matched horses were already in front of his phaeton.

The groom, Hopkins, who was on duty at night was just fastening the last of their harnesses.

"We're nearly finished, Your Grace," he said as he saw the Duke coming swiftly towards him.

"I want you to come with me," the Duke told him.

Hopkins stared at him.

"I haven't got my smart livery with me."

"That does not matter," the Duke answered. "Get in as you are and Travers will tell everyone we have left."

As he spoke, he slipped into the driver's seat and picked up the reins.

There was just time for Hopkins to snatch up his coat and hat which were certainly not smart livery, when the Duke started moving the horses.

As they had not been out for the last two days, they moved immediately into a fast pace and went down the drive with the dust swirling up behind them.

Fortunately the gates were open and the moonlight showed clearly that the road to the village was empty.

The Duke therefore set off at a pace which made Hopkins gasp for breath.

As they sped along, he wondered what could have happened to make the Duke drive faster than he had ever known him drive before.

As it was late at night and the road to London was almost empty, they arrived in what was record time.

The last star was fading in the sky and the first rays of the sun were appearing in the East.

It was seven o'clock in the morning when the Duke reached Penelope's house.

Handing the reins to Hopkins, he hammered on the door until it was opened by a surprised-looking housemaid.

"I wish to speak to Lady Penelope at once," he said walking in through the door which was only half-open.

"She ain't been called yet, sir," the maid told him.

"That does not matter," the Duke replied sharply, "I know the way."

The housemaid gasped as he hurried past her and started to climb the stairs, as she said afterwards, 'as only a madman would go up 'em.'

The Duke knew the way to Penelope's bedroom.

Without knocking he pushed the door open.

Penelope was in bed.

She had just opened her eyes but, because it was so early had closed them again.

Now as she heard heavy footsteps and someone approaching the bed, she opened her eyes and screamed when she saw it was a man.

"Who are you? What are you doing here?" she shrieked.

Then, as light from the side of the curtains showed her the Duke's face, she said,

"Ivan! What are you doing here?"

"I have come to see you," the Duke replied, "and you are going to tell me who you have paid or who you have told to kidnap Devinia and carry her away from The Castle."

He could see by the expression on Penelope's face that she knew what he was saying.

She pulled herself up on the pillows as she said,

"What has happened to Devinia is nothing at all to do with me."

"You are lying," he said accusingly. "You know as well as I do it was on your very instructions that she was captured by some foreigners and I suspect, again on your orders, she has been taken to a country where fair-haired women are exceedingly welcomed by a Czar or a Sultan who are always looking for them."

He was speaking harshly.

But he saw just for a moment a look of satisfaction in Penelope's eyes that what he had said was the truth.

It was what she had planned to be rid of Devinia.

"Come along," the Duke said angrily, "there is no time to waste! You will tell me where you have sent her or I suspect sold her."

"I just don't know what you are saying," Penelope replied. "In fact I think it is most insulting and you have no right to be here bursting into my bedroom before I have been called. I am sure that Papa will have a great deal to say on it."

"I am not concerned with your father or anyone else except you. Unless you tell me at once where you have sent Devinia I will make it very unpleasant for you."

"I really don't know what you are talking about," Penelope retorted, "and, if you want to tell me your silly ideas about Devinia, then you can wait until I have had breakfast. Then I will be delighted to entertain you."

"I thought you might take that attitude," the Duke answered. "As I know exactly what will happen to Devinia if she reaches one of those countries where the fair-haired women are appreciated, I demand that you tell me the truth now."

"And if I refuse to?" Penelope questioned.

"Then I will tell you what I intend to do," the Duke replied. "Because I am aware that Devinia would rather die than suffer as a concubine to some foreign devil, who would pay you for anything so revolting, I am determined that you shall tell me the truth."

Penelope tossed her head.

"And if I do not?" she enquired.

"Then I am going to make it impossible for you to look as attractive as you are at the moment and to be, as you believe, the most beautiful *debutante* in London."

As he spoke, he drew from his pocket a large knife and opened it.

"What are you saying? What are you doing?" she asked and there was now fear in her voice.

"I am saying that unless you tell me immediately where you have sent Devinia, I intend to make it quite impossible with the marks that will be on your cheeks for you ever again to be the most beautiful woman in London."

"What you are saying is nonsense – "

"I mean exactly what I am saying."

He opened the knife and now he took it in his hand.

"Tell me the truth where you have sent Devinia or I will mark your cheek in a way that will destroy your looks for ever."

Penelope drew in her breath.

Then, as the knife drew nearer to her, she said with almost a shriek,

"She has gone to – the Sultan in Istanbul. I hate you for treating me in this way."

"The Duke shut the knife and put it into his pocket.

"I think you are so despicable," he said, "that no decent man, if he knew what you had done, would ever speak to you again."

Penelope did not answer and he went on,

"As far as I am concerned that is what I feel about you. You are fortunate that I have not punished you as I should have by taking away your looks."

As he spoke, he walked out of the bedroom and slammed the door behind him.

In the hall there were quite a number of servants who had been roused by hearing that he had gone upstairs to Lady Penelope's room.

They did not try to stop him, but stared at him as he walked swiftly past them.

Climbing into his phaeton he said to Hopkins, who handed him the reins,

"Now we have to hurry!"

"Where are we goin', Your Grace?"

"To Dover," the Duke replied. "I intend to beat every record in getting there."

He almost snapped out the words.

Hopkins gulped as the horses sprang forward and turned into the main road.

'I'll be ever so surprised,' he thought to himself, 'if we get there alive.'

*

It was, however, midday when the Duke reached Dover.

Going to where his yacht was tied up, he found, as he expected, that the messenger from The Castle, by riding one of his fastest horses, had arrived there an hour earlier.

"You've not given us much time, Your Grace," the Captain said as he stepped aboard.

"I don't have very much time to spare," the Duke answered sharply. "Set to sea immediately, Captain."

"May I know where we're going?" he asked.

He spoke somewhat nervously as he was not used to seeing the Duke in such a strange mood.

"For the moment we are heading for the Bay of Biscay and then to the Mediterranean," the Duke informed him. "Later I will tell you exactly where I want to land and I only hope that you are as fast as I have always believed you to be."

He spoke in such a way that the Captain stared at him.

Then the Duke turned back to thank Hopkins and to give him orders to take the horses back to The Castle as quietly and easily as possible.

He then returned to his yacht and told the Captain,

"Full steam ahead!"

The Captain did as he was told.

Only when they were in the English Channel did the Duke say to Captain Davenport,

"Did you notice, and I know you are very sharp-eyed where ships are concerned, if there was one leaving early this morning. It would probably have been flying the flag of the Ottoman Empire."

The Captain wrinkled his brow before he said,

"Now you mention it there was a ship leaving about eight o'clock. As you so rightly say it has always been my interest to count the ships which are in harbour and wonder if they can move as swiftly as I can."

He laughed at his own joke.

But, as the Duke's face was unmoved, he said,

"Yes, Your Grace, you are right. There was one ship and now I think about it, I am sure that it was carrying the flag of the Ottoman Empire."

He hesitated before he added,

"I also seem to remember it had a crew of natives."

"That is what I want to know," the Duke answered.

Going into his own cabin, he closed the door and Captain Davenport stared after him with a puzzled look on his face.

'I suppose once we get to sea he'll tell me what all this is about,' he said to himself. 'It was very lucky that we were ready to move so quickly and that I took on board yesterday enough food and fuel and everything else we are likely to need on what might be a long voyage.'

He gave a sigh as he added to himself,

'Thank goodness I have not been caught napping.'

CHAPTER SIX

When Devinia had felt the blankets falling over her, she had fought with both hands to keep them off her face.

Then, as she felt herself lifted up, she realised with a growing sense of horror that she was being kidnapped.

For a moment she could not believe that what she was thinking was true.

She tried again to push the blankets away from her face and then, as she realised that she was being carried by men, perhaps there were four of them, she knew that she had no chance of winning however hard she struggled.

She tried to think clearly where they had come from and what they were doing, but without any enlightenment.

Then she found herself dumped into the back of a carriage and she thought that she must be on the back seat.

As the horses started off, she realised that she was being carried away from The Castle.

Where were they going?

Where was she being taken?

The questions ran through her mind and repeated and repeated themselves.

Then, as she heard the men talking and speaking a language that she knew was foreign, she was aware that this was all part of a plot.

She was being taken out of England simply because in that way she could not be with the Duke.

It just seemed impossible and incredible.

Yet as they travelled on she became more and more convinced that this was Penelope's doing.

On her instructions, or rather her arrangements, she was being taken from the Duke in a manner which would ensure absolutely that he would never see her again.

'How could this happen to me?' Devinia asked.

And yet it was happening and there was nothing she could do about it.

'How could anyone be so cruel as to do this to me?' she whispered to herself.

But the answer was right there clearly and she had to accept it.

She had taken the Duke away from Penelope and now Penelope was having her revenge.

Who else would have known that a dog whining in pain would have brought her straight out of her room and downstairs and then outside to see what was happening?

Who else, except Penelope, would want her to be taken away to some foreign land so that the Duke would never find her?

The whole horror of it swept over her and now she was praying fervently for help.

'Help me, God, please, please help me! Save me from these horrible men!'

Then, as she was so desperately afraid and because she felt so helpless, she called out to the Duke.

Calling him with her mind and her body and most of all her fear of what lay ahead for her.

"Help me! Help me!" she kept calling out over and over again, but there was no one to hear her.

She then remembered how some times the Duke seemed to read her mind and to know what she was about to say before she even said it.

Then she told herself that the whole situation was impossible.

How could the Duke know she had been carried away? If he had been aware of it, he would have appeared before she was actually covered up and carried by the men to their carriage.

Perhaps they would drive on for hours and hours before they finally came to a standstill.

'This just cannot be true, this cannot be happening to me,' she screamed in her mind.

She wondered whether she was being taken away to a house, a prison or some strange place that she had never heard of.

And then to her surprise she was lifted out of the carriage and the four men were carrying her over stony ground.

Then what she thought, although it really seemed impossible, was a smooth hard surface that might be wood.

Then suddenly so that she gave a little scream, she was picked up and she realised that the men were carrying her into a ship.

As if to confirm her impression, she next heard the sound of another ship in the distance.

She could now hear the engines throbbing as if they were impatient to put to sea.

To Devinia, it was all almost like a nightmare that there was no awakening from.

Then suddenly she was put down and, although she could not see where she was, she was almost certain that it was a cabin aboard a ship.

'Where are they taking me? Oh, God save me!' she prayed. 'Why am I being taken away from my country? Oh please, please, Ivan, save me! Save me! *Save me*!'

The words throbbed in her forehead.

Then she kept repeating them, although now when she was aware that the ship was moving beneath her, it was hard to breathe.

The weight of the blankets which covered her had made her breathless ever since she had left The Castle.

Now she hoped that they would be removed or else she might suffocate and die.

For a few moments she thought even that would be better than being kept a prisoner of these people, whoever they were, who had carried her away.

Then, as if her mother and father were speaking to her, she recognised that she must be brave.

Whatever was happening she must meet it with her usual confidence and belief that, if she was in danger, God would send someone to help her.

'Help me! *Please* help me!'

Again she was crying out in her mind to the Duke.

It was then that she heard footsteps near her and was aware that two people, she thought they must be men, were removing the blankets covering her.

Because she thought it wise, she lay very still and did not try to move even when the last blanket was pulled away.

She found herself lying, as she had thought that she was, in the cabin of a ship.

Then she was aware that the two men at her head and the man at her feet, were natives.

She tried to guess what nationality they were.

She knew that they were not French nor Italian, but came from the East.

She stared at them and then realised that they were staring at her.

Then one man, who seemed to be older than the others and had, she thought, something about him which made him appear to be better bred or more educated said,

"You all right? You not hurt?"

He was speaking to her in broken English and she answered him by saying,

"No, I am not hurt. But I want to know why you have carried me away and – who you are working for?"

She spoke slowly and distinctly as she was sure that otherwise he would not understand what she said.

To her surprise he replied,

"You be told everything later, but not now."

Now that she could see him more clearly, he was dark-skinned and came from a country that she still could not put a name to.

With an effort she sat up and the man asked her,

"You hot? You want drink of water?"

"Yes, please," she replied. "I was very hot under all those blankets"

She looked at what had enveloped her and saw that they were Eastern looking as the material was rough.

But she had to admit that they were clean and had not, she thought, been used before she had been enveloped in them.

Slowly and a little unsteadily she rose to her feet.

By this time the ship was out at sea and moving roughly through the waves.

To save herself she caught hold of the bed and realised that, as it was not a berth and attached to the wall, it was actually a bed in the middle of the cabin.

This told her that she was in the main cabin of the ship that she was travelling in or, as the English would call it, 'the Master cabin'.

She stood against the bed as she demanded,

"Where are you taking me?"

"The Captain tell you all later," the man who spoke English answered.

Then, picking up the blankets that had covered her, they went from the cabin closing the door behind them.

Then Devinia was aware that the key had been in the lock.

By this time the ship was moving quicker and still quicker and she went to the basin to wash her face and her hands.

There were clean towels and, after she had washed, she felt a little better, but she was still desperately afraid as to where she was being taken.

The cabin, although it contained a bed, was not that large and she thought that it was furnished and decorated in a foreign fashion and not what one would have expected from an English owner.

Because it was hot she took off her dressing gown.

Feeling that there was nothing else she could do, she got into the bed.

It was clean, but the bedclothes were rough and smelt musty and certainly would not have been accepted by any English owner of a ship.

She was thinking how desperately thirsty she was and hoped that the man, who had asked her if she would like a drink, had not forgotten, when the key in the lock was turned and someone knocked on the door.

"Come in," Devinia called out.

A man who was obviously a servant, came into the cabin carrying a tray, a jug, and a glass and what she hoped was lemonade.

He set the tray with its contents down beside her on the bed and said,

"You want more – ring bell."

He spoke hesitantly as if each word was difficult.

Then before she could reply he went quickly out of the cabin shutting the door and locking it behind him.

Devinia found that the drink was indeed lemonade and she drank a little of it which took some of the dryness from her throat.

By now the ship was well out to sea.

She could only wonder apprehensively where it was going and who had snatched her away from The Castle and from everything she knew and loved.

And she could not help hoping that they would not forget Prince and someone would feed him in her absence.

Then once again she was thinking of the Duke and feeling that he must be wondering where she was.

She could only hope and pray that he was thinking of rescuing her.

'Come to me! *Come to me*!' she called to him.

When there was no reply, she felt for the first time the tears of fear coming into her eyes.

The ship must have been well down the English Channel before there was a knock on the door, which was very different from the rather timid one that she had heard before.

"Come in," Devinia said, sitting up in bed.

She wondered who her visitor could possibly be.

When he appeared, she knew at once from the way he was dressed and the way he walked, that he was the Captain of this ship and well aware of his position.

As he came to the bed, she realised that, if she was eyeing him anxiously, he was doing the same.

"Are you comfortable?" he asked abruptly in a way that showed he spoke English well and could understand it.

"Yes, I am comfortable, thank you," Devinia said. "But you will understand that I wish to know where I am going and who this ship belongs to?"

The Captain smiled.

"You be quite safe," he said. "We look after you well. You a present for His Highness."

"And who is – His Highness?" Devinia asked.

For a short moment there was hesitation and then the Captain answered,

"He very great man, the Sultan of Istanbul, and you a present to him."

Devinia drew in her breath. Now she understood exactly what had happened to her.

There was no doubt as to who had arranged it.

When Devinia had been with her mother's cousin, Penelope's father was negotiating on behalf of the Sultan of Istanbul over a ship he was having made in England.

Apparently, although she had not heard of it before, Penelope's father was an acclaimed expert on the building and equipping of cargo boats and had received orders from many countries for those made in English shipyards.

Because she had been interested he had told her of the number of ships he had built for different countries and the many ways that they had been furnished if they were to carry passengers.

"The majority," he had told her, "require only ships that convey what they buy in one country to their own, but occasionally the Sultan or whoever is important, wants one for his own personal use."

He paused for a moment and then continued,

"That, I can assure you, makes a lot of difficulties because, although he admires our furniture and our form of decoration, he also wants it to be partially Eastern and that, of course, causes problems not only where he is concerned but for the guests of his country."

Devinia had listened attentively because anything new was interesting for her.

She particularly wanted to know how the countries that had a Sultan differed from those that had a King.

She was therefore surprised when the Captain said,

"This ship belongs to the Sultan of Istanbul and he uses it to bring the English to his country and to make them comfortable during the journey."

The way he spoke made Devinia understand all too clearly that the Sultan of Istanbul had copied the English in some ways.

However there was definitely a foreign touch where the bedclothes were concerned and Devinia was to find out later that the majority of the food and furniture on board was very Oriental.

But what she had heard already was enough for her to realise all too clearly what Penelope had planned for her.

She was quite certain that, as her father's daughter, it would be easy for her to have someone carried aboard the Sultan's ship if it was in harbour at Dover and there was no reason for her to consult her father.

Devinia guessed that, while he was busy inspecting the ships that were being made under his orders, Penelope had sent the men from the ship to kidnap her and to take her aboard without her father having the least idea of what was happening.

There was no need for Devinia to ask the Captain why she should have been taken for the Sultan of Istanbul.

Her father had often talked about the present Sultan who he saw quite often.

On more than one time he had teased his daughter by saying if she became even more famous than she was already as a beautiful *debutante*, the Sultan would hear of her beauty and, as he had a penchant for blondes, would undoubtedly send a ship to carry her to him in Istanbul.

She really could not believe that any Englishman, especially one accepted by the most influential people in London, would capture an English girl and then, because she was fair, send her to the Sultan.

But that was exactly what Penelope was doing.

While she was using her father's name to make it possible, it was very doubtful if he would learn what had happened, at any rate not until it was too late to rescue her.

"We make you very comfortable," the Captain was saying. "You just ask for anything you want and we go straight to Istanbul and not stop anywhere."

Devinia knew that it was no use appealing to him to save her from the fate that awaited her when she arrived.

But he was well aware that she was a present for the Sultan and so she would be added to his harem, which according to Penelope's father was already a large one.

When the Captain left after again saying that she had only to ask for anything she wanted, Devinia lay down.

She told herself that if she was not rescued then she must die before she was made one of the Sultan's many concubines simply because she was so fair and fair-haired women were more to his liking than dark girls who were of the same blood as his own.

'Help me, God! Please help me!' Devinia prayed.

But she could not think how God could do so. Or how once they had passed through the Mediterranean and reached Istanbul, there would be anyone she could appeal to to save her.

As the ship seemed to go faster and faster, she told herself that, if neither God nor the Duke heard her prayers, then she must die.

When finally that night she fell asleep, she felt as if the Devil himself was carrying her towards a Hell she had not thought existed until this moment.

*

The Duke, having ordered that his yacht should sail night and day as fast as it possibly could, was calculating that, as far as he was concerned, Devinia had left ten or more hours earlier than he had done.

He had, of course, lost time when he had gone first to London to see Penelope.

He had then driven at what was an amazing speed to Dover, only to be quite certain that Devinia was several hours ahead of him.

As he had travelled so much in the past, he was well aware of the fascination that Eastern men felt for fair-haired, blue-eyed English girls, who often, when they went abroad unprotected, found themselves in a most unpleasant situation.

They had, of course, no idea how they could save themselves.

He had been friendly with the Sultan of Istanbul who he had met on several occasions and thought him a well-educated and, on the whole, intelligent man.

At the same time he was well aware that he boasted a very large harem.

It was talked about not only in the East but in many other countries where the Sultan was not only a visitor but accepted by a great number of other Rulers as being a man who was making Istanbul, over which he ruled, far more advanced physically and intellectually than a good number of other Eastern countries.

But they had remained somewhat hostile towards Europeans.

It was well known that the Sultan of Istanbul had a penchant for fair girls and it was no secret that he collected them as other Rulers might collect weapons or jewels.

But to think of Devinia being a concubine of the Sultan was something that made the Duke's blood boil and want to kill anyone who prevented him from saving her.

But he was clever enough to realise that it was not going to be an easy task to save Devinia from the Sultan.

He would need to use all his brains as well as his charm, unless he was not only to lose her but every respect he had for himself.

'How could I have possibly thought, how could I have guessed for one moment,' he asked himself a million times, 'that Penelope would punish me in such a manner for insulting her and how could Devinia have thought it dangerous to go to an injured dog outside my Castle.'

All these questions kept forcing themselves into his mind until he thought that he would go mad if he could not catch up with the Sultan's ship ahead of him.

He was well aware, as the Captain had pointed out to Devinia, that the Sultan's ship was a larger vessel.

Thanks to the Company who had built it under the supervision of Penelope's father, it had engines, which if required could go very fast especially with a small cargo.

And much faster than the Duke's yacht.

"You just have to move quicker than you are at the moment," the Duke told his Captain, "simply because it is a matter of life and death. I have to reach Istanbul, if it is at all possible, before the Sultan's ship ahead of us goes in to Port."

"We can only hope, Your Grace," the Captain said, "that they stop to refuel or to buy food. Otherwise we will be a day or perhaps two days behind them."

"You just have to go faster," the Duke urged him.

Without waiting for the Captain to reply, he walked on deck as if he hoped to see the Sultan's ship ahead.

There were a great number of ships at Gibraltar and Marseilles and also at Naples.

The Captain did not stop at these Ports. He and the Duke merely inspected them through binoculars.

They made quite certain each time that there was no sign of the Sultan's ship and it was still ahead of them.

*

If the Duke was regretting that the Sultan's ship was moving so quickly, Devinia was feeling the same.

She was aware that it was most unusual for a ship carrying friends or guests to sail on without stopping so that they could sleep quietly at night in a small bay.

It was also usual to pick up fresh water and food and, of course, to refuel at regular intervals.

The Sultan's ship moved ahead rapidly.

To Devinia and the Duke following her, it was the luck of the Devil that they had no reason to stop.

When they entered the Aegean Sea, it was early in the morning.

When they docked in the Port of Istanbul, it was well before the average person's breakfast time.

"There is no reason for you to hurry," the Captain said to Devinia. "As soon as we arrive, I will send to The Palace to inform them that you are here and they will send a carriage for you."

"I must point out to you," Devinia said, "that I have no clothes and I have no wish to arrive in my nightgown which is how I was taken away and why, ever since I came aboard, I have not left this bed."

The Captain threw up his hand in a typical gesture of helplessness.

"How could we know when we were not told until we reached England that a beautiful lady like yourself, who was to be taken to His Highness the Sultan, would have no luggage with her?"

Devinia did not wish to argue and did not point out that she was lured downstairs by the yelping of a dog that they were torturing and then carried away.

"So I will tell those at The Palace that you require clothes before you leave ship," he said.

"Thank you," Devinia replied.

She wished that she could think of a reason to delay her arrival still further.

But it took two hours before two women arrived with a large box containing the clothes that they thought Devinia should wear.

She lay in bed as she watched them unpack what they had brought and, because she had no wish to meet the Sultan, she refused most of the clothes they offered her.

She was only persuaded with great difficulty which took time, before she finally dressed herself in the Eastern fashion.

She wore a veil so that only her eyes were showing when eventually she condescended to leave the ship.

Even then she sat in the ship's Saloon for a long time talking to the Captain.

She told him that she was hoping the Sultan would be kind enough to let her return home to England and she knew, even as she spoke to him, that he was quite certain she would not be allowed to do so.

At least it gave her a chance to express her feelings at being kidnapped and being forced as an Englishwoman into the Sultan's harem.

"It is a disgrace to my country," Devinia said. "I am hoping that the Sultan will be reprimanded by Her Majesty Queen Victoria for behaving in such a disgraceful way."

She had not said all this when he had come to see her aboard the ship for the simple reason that she had felt weak lying in bed, while he merely asked her if she was comfortable and if there was anything she required.

Now dressed, even though it was as a native, she felt stronger in herself.

Although she thought miserably it would do her no good, she was determined to let the Captain know that she thought he and the Sultan were behaving appallingly.

She was well aware as she was talking to him that he was thinking of asserting his authority and making her leave immediately as the carriage was waiting.

"You understand," he said, "I only take orders from His Highness the Sultan. If he say bring lady to Istanbul, I have to bring you. If I don't do what I'm told, I'm thrown out, finished – you understand?"

"I understand exactly," Devinia said coldly. "At the same time I am shocked that in the world today the people of Istanbul should behave like *barbarians*."

As she said the last word, she then walked down the gangway, her head held high, and stepped into the carriage.

To her surprise there was a woman inside it.

Not one of the women who had brought her clothes as they were in a different carriage, but an elderly woman who spoke very little English.

She was there, Devinia discovered, to point out the places of interest in the City as they passed through it.

And to inform her, in case she was upset, that the Sultan was away and did not return until late that night.

Devinia did not make a comment but her heart leapt in case, although it would be a miracle, there was a way of saving herself before he arrived.

She had to admit, although she would not say so aloud, that the City was very attractive in the sunshine

She could see many colourful shops and she had a feeling of satisfaction she could not explain as there also seemed to be very few beggars or badly dressed children.

The horses and dogs, and there were quite a number of them, were obviously well fed and not harshly treated.

The Sultan's Palace was only a short way outside the main City of Istanbul and the olive trees surrounding it made it look enchanting.

There were quite a number of people waiting to greet Devinia as she stepped out of the carriage, hoping that she looked confident and at the same time dignified.

Only to herself did she acknowledge that her lips were dry and her heart was beating rapidly with fear.

With much bowing she was led into the Palace, but not through the main door, but one which she soon realised was used by those who were the Sultan's concubines.

As she knew that the Sultan was away, she was not so frightened as she would have been otherwise.

She was also well aware that the elderly women who were to look after her, were bowing and scraping as if she was an English Princess rather than just a girl whose most important attribute was her golden hair.

She was taken to a bedroom that she had to admit looked comfortable and larger than she expected and she was shown a sitting room opening out of it which she was told she would share with two of the Sultan's favourites.

One of them was a German who was fair and the other, Devinia gathered, was from Southern Russia.

As neither could speak a word of English, she felt that their conversation would be somewhat limited.

But they were obviously anxious to be pleasant and they bowed and smiled in a manner, which made it very obvious that they were anxious to welcome her.

She went into her bedroom and found, as she might have expected, that the wardrobe was full of clothes, all of Oriental style. They were attractive and not in any way degrading.

When she was asked if she had any jewellery, she replied that she had been taken away at night and brought to Istanbul with nothing of her own, except her nightgown.

This was explained with the help of a woman who spoke good English.

She had been, Devinia learnt later, a Governess at one of the Universities where some of the pupils required foreign languages as they hoped to work with Companies in England and America.

"You are very lucky to come here," the woman told Devinia. "Our Sultan like English girls very much."

She did not answer her, but later she was told that the Sultan had three Palaces and this one was his Summer Palace.

It was then she learnt that she was to have lessons in how to approach the Sultan and how he expected her to make love to him.

It was with difficulty that Devinia prevented herself from saying that it was something she would never do.

In fact she would rather die than attempt it.

But because she was sensible she forced herself to listen while the Teacher told her how the Sultan expected his concubines to start by kissing his feet and rise gently up until they had the great privilege of making love with him.

There was nothing that Devinia could say or do but listen, but every nerve in her body told her that this could never happen to her.

She would much rather die than be degraded into attempting such a performance.

"Tomorrow I will tell you more," the Teacher said. "But now it is time for us to have what you call 'dinner'. Then, as you travelled a long way to come here, you go to bed and sleep peacefully. Tomorrow His Highness may send for you or he may wait for another day. If he too tired, he sleep alone. We wait for our instructions."

It was with difficulty that Devinia prevented herself from saying she had no intention of taking any instructions.

Then, as she was taken to the dining room, she was wondering desperately how she could die and how it was possible to kill herself without all these women preventing her from doing so.

After dinner had finished, Devinia said that she was tired and wished to go to bed.

Only when she was in her own room, which was small but at least comfortable, did she put her hands over her eyes and asked herself despairingly how she could kill herself rather than follow the instructions of the woman who had talked to her.

'Please God, let me die!' she prayed.

Then, as if she could not help herself, she called out fervently again and again for the Duke.

'Ivan! *Ivan*!' she pleaded. 'Hear me. You said you could read what I was thinking, but I want you, I want you!

Only you can save me now. Otherwise I must die and I do not really want to die. I want to live and to be with you. Oh, Ivan, hear me.'

Her tears prevented her from praying anymore.

As she lay in the darkness, she felt that there was no future for her.

Only death could ever save her from the horror and misery that was waiting for her.

*

As it happened, the Duke's yacht was only a little way behind the ship carrying Devinia.

As they moved into Port, he saw it a little way from where they were dropping anchor.

Without waiting for protocol or going, as he might have done, to the British Embassy, the Duke went straight to The Palace and demanded to see the Sultan.

The Equerry who attended to him was impressed by his title and he was also aware that the Duke had called on the Sultan on previous occasions.

"His Highness will be back late tonight," he said, "and I know he will be delighted to hear that Your Grace is in Istanbul. In the summer he has breakfast very early at seven o'clock and usually deals with his post afterwards."

"Very well," the Duke said, "I will call just before eight o'clock."

"As you might know, this is the Summer Palace," the Equerry went on, "and he spends a great deal of time here."

"Very wise. I will be sleeping on my yacht tonight and will, as you suggest, call on His Highness tomorrow."

"That will be fine. I expect Your Grace knows, His Highness always says, as he finishes his business, 'now I can enjoy myself,' and it is what we try to do for him."

"That is very sensible," the Duke agreed.

He longed to ask him if Devinia was here and if she was being properly looked after.

But he knew that it would be a mistake for anyone to think of them as being together.

So he must wait until tomorrow before it would be possible to say anything to her or to ask if he could see her.

As he drove back to the Port, the Duke was almost praying that he would act cleverly and not, on any account, make a mistake that might harm Devinia.

'I have to save her,' he said to himself.

It was what he repeated over and over again later in his cabin before he fell into a troubled sleep.

CHAPTER SEVEN

The Duke arrived at The Palace at a quarter to eight and learnt from the Equerry in charge that the Sultan had just finished his breakfast and was going into the garden.

"His Highness would never miss a chance of being amongst his flowers," the Equerry said conversationally.

The Duke smiled.

He remembered only too well the Sultan's passion for flowers and he had in the past often teased him about it.

They had become friends at one of the numerous Conferences which were always taking place in Europe.

Actually it was held in Istanbul and he had attended as he had been asked by the British Ambassador to go to help as he not only spoke several languages but had made friends with people from many countries during his travels.

"You have been such a help with some of the more difficult representatives," the Ambassador told him.

The Duke had made a grimace.

"That is all that you really want me for," he replied, "and I find them as difficult as you do!"

"Yes," the Ambassador agreed. "But you can speak their language and you have visited their countries. Quite frankly I cannot do without you."

As the Duke had always been great friends with the Ambassador, he knew that he was not exaggerating when he said how difficult the world's Rulers could be.

He had indeed attended not one but quite a number of meetings with various countries and each of them fought for what they believed was their rights.

At the same time the Duke enjoyed himself simply because he did know a great deal about the less significant countries concerned.

He thought it only fair that they should have their chance of expressing their thoughts and feelings as well as the bigger and more powerful countries.

Because he enjoyed visiting Istanbul he had a large knowledge of its history and he had enjoyed meeting the new Sultan and learning of the improvements he meant to make in the country that he now ruled over.

They had in fact become friends and on his journey from England the Duke had thought over and over again that the only hope of him saving Devinia was the fact that he knew the Sultan personally.

Had it been any other country he was quite certain if she had been carried off in such a blatant manner with the permission of one of her relations, it would have been extremely difficult to ask for her to be given back.

He might have come up against a blank wall where they protested firmly that what he was saying was untrue and there was no question of him saving her.

All the same he realised that it was an exceedingly difficult situation as he was certain that Penelope would have used her father's name to give them permission to kidnap Devinia.

What was more she was, as he knew only too well, exactly the fair blue-eyed golden-haired beauty who every man in Istanbul would admire and wish to possess.

The Equerry brought the Duke a cold drink while he was waiting and he told him about the improvements that the Sultan had already made in Istanbul.

"We are getting larger every year," he said. "More people come to buy products from us and His Highness is very pleased that there are so many English visitors."

"I am glad to hear that," the Duke replied. "I am delighted to be here in Istanbul as I have always thought it to be one of the most attractive countries I have visited."

The Equerry smiled and then he said,

"I will go and see if His Highness is in the garden and tell him that you are here, Your Grace, I am sure that he will be very pleased to hear of it."

He left the room closing the door behind him.

As if he could not keep still, the Duke rose from his chair and walked to the window.

He could not see the trees in the garden because he was concentrating with all his heart and soul on winning the battle that he was well aware lay ahead of him.

'I have to be clever and I have to be sensible,' he told himself, 'and I must not in any way to incur his anger.'

Then, as he heard he Equerry return, for a moment he did not turn round, he only drew in his breath.

In his heart he said the same prayer as he had said all the way as he sailed down the Mediterranean.

He knew that, once a woman had passed into the keeping of the Sultan, it was almost impossible for her to leave or be taken back into her family.

"If you would please come this way, Your Grace," the Equerry was saying. "I told His Highness you are here and he is delighted to welcome you."

The Duke turned and walked behind the Equerry, who took him to the door that led into the garden.

He threw open the door and there was no reason for the Equerry to take him any further as the Duke had seen on his last visit where the Sultan would be sitting.

It should have been a tent, but it was more like an elaborate and canopied bed.

Now, as he had expected, the Sultan was lying back against his silk cushions.

He was wearing so little clothing that it was quite obvious what was expected later on.

As the Duke appeared, the Sultan lifted both his arms and exclaimed,

"Your Grace! I did not expect to see you here."

"I came to see you, Your Highness."

There was a chair at the Sultan's side and the Duke sat down in it saying as he did so,

"I must apologise for my unexpected visit, but it is of great importance to me. I am extremely grateful to Your Highness for seeing me at such short notice."

"Of course I want to see you," the Sultan replied. "I have often thought about you and how we used to laugh at that last meeting. You made that stupid and idiotic man from France look more of a fool than he was already!"

The Duke chuckled.

"That was true enough. Of course, you won, as I remember, exactly what you wanted at the time and I heard from your Equerry that things are going extremely well in Istanbul at the moment."

"We are now making good money," the Sultan said waving his hands, "and who could ask for more?"

"Who indeed?" the Duke questioned, "they must be very proud of you. As I recall when you took over, things were very bad and people were leaving the City because they could not afford to stay in it."

"Now they are coming back," the Sultan said, "and we have had many visitors including some from England."

There was a pause and then the Duke said,

"It is about someone who has been brought to you from England that I wish to talk to you about. She did not intend to come and visit you, but there is every likelihood that I would have brought her here later on."

The Sultan looked at him in surprise.

"What are you talking about?" he enquired.

"I am talking about a young girl who your people were asked to kidnap and bring to you against her will and against mine."

The Sultan stared at him.

"Of course I know who you are talking about," he said, "but I had no idea that it concerned you in any way."

The Duke smiled.

"It concerns me for the simple reason, and I know you will understand, we are engaged to be married and I intend to make her my wife."

The Sultan glared at the Duke and replied,

"This cannot be true! I cannot believe what you are saying to me. It must be a joke which I do *not* find funny."

"Nor do I," the Duke answered. "The situation is quite simple. You know, as we both discussed it on my last visit, that I had no intention of marrying. I intended to be getting on for forty before I gave up my freedom and then only because I needed an heir."

"Yes, yes," the Sultan replied. "I do remember you saying that. We both agreed that the bonds of matrimony could be very tiresome."

He paused before he went on,

"I remember relating to you that my predecessor suffered terribly from an older woman who he took as his Consort and he bitterly regretted her doing so."

"I have not forgotten," the Duke replied. "That is why, when I learnt of the terrible and ghastly trick that has been played on me, I have come to you for justice and understanding."

The Sultan waved his hands.

"I don't understand. Tell me what happened."

"You remember buying your private yacht from a man who specialises in providing them in Great Britain," the Duke began, "and in fact I think I told you to ask for his help when you wanted English furnishings and engines that would move faster than any other private yacht in this part of the world."

"Yes, yes, I remember," the Sultan answered rather impatiently.

"Unfortunately," the Duke went on, "the maker you employed has a beautiful daughter, who was much admired and applauded when she became a *debutante* last year. In consequence she became very sure of herself and decided that she would marry a title."

The Sultan laughed.

"So her eyes rested on you, Your Grace, and she wanted to be your wife."

"Exactly!" he replied. "But as you know only too well because you and I discussed it, I had no wish to marry and I decided, and I think you said the same, we would both wait until we were older and wiser."

He smiled as he added,

"Our age, if nothing else, would prevent us from being bullied by our wives!"

The Sultan laughed again.

"Of course, we said that. I remember only too well that I was being hotly pursued by a woman I found most unattractive."

"I might say the same. I had no wish to marry that particular lady, but then by chance I met a young unspoilt girl who was being very badly treated."

"So, you broke your resolution," the Sultan said.

"I thought you would guess it," the Duke laughed. "She is young, unspoilt and not in the least demanding."

He sighed.

"So I gave her an engagement ring and thought that I was at last marrying a woman who would not want to order me around or be more interested in my title than in me."

"What happened then?" the Sultan asked as if he was eager to know the whole story.

"The woman who wanted to have her own way and that included me," the Duke went on, "asked your men to kidnap my beautiful fiancée and carry her away, which she least expected, so that she could become a member of your harem."

The Sultan stared at him.

"Is this true?" he demanded. "Is it possible that this girl you are engaged to has been kidnapped by my men?"

"She is here in your Palace," the Duke confirmed, "but I have been told as you have been away that you have not yet seen her."

The Sultan did not reply and he carried on,

"But I must beg you, as a friend and a man who understands these difficulties where women are concerned, to let me have her back."

The Sultan put his hand up to his forehead.

"It all seems to me impossible. How would they dare to kidnap an English girl and bring her here without causing a great deal of trouble? Are you quite sure that she was not anxious to join me?"

"She did not know what was happening," the Duke replied. "She was enticed from her bed because a dog was whining in apparent pain beneath her window."

He paused for a moment before he continued,

"She is very fond of all animals as you know most English women are and she went down in her nightgown to see what was happening."

"And what did she find?" the Sultan asked.

"Before she could speak and before she could even find the dog," the Duke told him, "she was covered with blankets until it was almost impossible for her to breathe. She was carried away by four men to a carriage which was waiting just around the corner from my Castle."

The Sultan was listening but he did not interrupt.

"She did not know why it was happening nor was she able to speak until she found herself aboard your ship. So I have followed her as swiftly as I could because she is to be my wife."

The Sultan did not reply and the Duke went on,

"If it is learnt by the Diplomatic Service, or indeed the Government, that she has been kidnapped then it might lead to difficult relations between our two countries. That is a situation I know, my friend, is what you and I would wish to avoid."

"I still cannot believe that my people would be so stupid as to steal your fiancée," the Sultan asserted.

He spoke in French because at their last meeting there had been many French Officers and they had often conversed with them in their own language.

"I think," the Duke said quietly, "that your people believed that the order came direct from the man who built your ship. Therefore they did not query it."

He hesitated slightly before he added,

"Equally it was a dangerous thing to do and I think, if you will forgive me saying so, it would be wise if you told them that in the future they must not kidnap English women however much they are paid to do so, unless they have instructions from you or an Officer on your behalf."

"You are right, of course, you are right!" the Sultan agreed. "But now she is in my harem, what can I do about it?"

This was what the Duke had expected and he said,

"But I can only beg you to give her back to me. I thought it would make it easier for you to bargain with me if, when you return my future wife, I gave you something which everyone in the East, who is important like yourself, would really like."

As he spoke he drew the necklace of opals out of his pocket.

"This was made by my great-great-grandfather who found the stones in China. He then had them made into a necklace with, as you can see, diamonds and pearls."

The Sultan was looking at it with great interest and the Duke went on,

"The diamonds are particularly fine and if you wear anything so magnificent at the next meeting to be held in the East, you will be the envy of every Potentate."

As he spoke, he slipped the necklace over his own head and it fell, as he intended, firmly onto his shoulders.

At the end of it there was a large circle of jewels surrounding an extremely large opal in the centre.

Having put it on, the Duke stood up.

The Sultan gave a gasp at the way it made him look so charismatic and he knew that the wearer would be the envy of everyone who looked at him.

"As I have already told you," the Duke said, "this was made by my ancestor two centuries ago. But those who followed him were always too shy to wear it."

He smiled as he added,

"I believe that it would make you look even more important that you do already, especially at a meeting such as we both attended last year."

Just for a moment the Sultan hesitated.

Then as if the lure of the beautiful necklace was too much for him to resist, he said,

"You must be very much in love, my dear friend, if you would sacrifice anything quite so sublime in return for a woman."

Very slowly the Duke took the necklace off himself and, bending down, he placed it on the Sultan's shoulders.

"Now you will be the envy of everyone you know," he said. "But all I can do is to beg you to see that it is carefully looked after, so that it cannot be stolen. It is unique and no one else has ever found so many opals or to my knowledge had them encased in a necklace."

"You are right, it is unique," the Sultan agreed. "I can only hope, my dear friend, that your sacrifice for this woman will make you happy."

"At the next Conference that we attend, I will look forward to seeing you wearing this necklace," the Duke replied, "and thank you, thank you from the bottom of my heart for giving me what I am really anxious to have. That is a wife who loves me for myself who will give me sons to carry on my name when I die."

"I really cannot believe that any woman, however beautiful, is as valuable as this necklace," the Sultan said, speaking as if to himself rather than the Duke.

Looking up at the Duke, he added,

"The woman you speak about must be special and different from all the others either of us have met. Perhaps I am making a mistake in losing her."

"And you would be making an even bigger mistake if you lose the necklace, which I hope when you die you will leave to your eldest son and your successor in Istanbul. He will wear it until he can pass it on to his son."

"You are right," the Sultan murmured. "There is no one else who will have anything so stupendous to wear."

"You will be much admired, much envied and, of course, they will try to copy you," the Duke said. "But they will find it very difficult. Those sort of stones do not exist today or, if they do, you and I have not found them."

He had not sat down again and now he held out his hand.

"Goodbye, my friend. I am most grateful to you and you have done me a great service. If ever you want me, I will, of course, come at once."

"I am grateful to you," the Sultan replied covering the Duke's hand with both of his. "If you will tell me when your Wedding will be, I will send you a Wedding present although it will not be a necklace as wonderful as this."

"Any present you send me, Your Highness, will be received gratefully and will be much admired."

There was a pause before he added,

"Goodbye again and may you one day discover the same happiness that I have found, although, as you know only too well, it is a difficult thing to find."

The Sultan laughed.

"Goodbye, Your Grace, and I will tell my Equerry that the last arrival from England is to return with you."

"I am more grateful than I can say in words," the Duke responded.

He then bowed, as was expected of him and walked to the door.

It was opened by the Equerry and the Duke said,

"His Highness has some instructions for you."

He went into The Palace without looking back and waited until the Equerry returned.

"I will tell the English lady," he said, "that you are waiting for her."

"We have to leave in a hurry," the Duke answered.

Without replying the Equerry then hurried down the passage.

The Duke drew in his breath.

He realised that he had achieved the impossible in getting Devinia freed once she had actually been accepted into the Sultan's Palace.

Yet as he waited he glanced at the closed door into the garden in case he was being too optimistic and things were not as easy as he thought they were.

Finally he heard voices and knew that Devinia was coming to him.

He looked out and saw that his carriage had been brought round to the front door and was waiting outside.

Everything was going smoothly.

Yet the Duke knew that no one could be certain of anything in the East. Rulers like the Sultan changed their minds as swiftly and as often as the air changed.

Then, when he was becoming somewhat anxious that something had gone wrong, Devinia appeared.

She was wearing the clothes she had been dressed in to meet the Sultan.

Although they were very pretty and colourful, they hardly covered her body.

They were, the Duke knew, deliberately seductive to accentuate the fairness beneath them.

Even though she was looking extremely pretty, the Duke knew by the expression in her eyes that she was very frightened.

As she saw him, she gave a cry which seemed to come from the very depths of her soul.

She ran towards him and threw herself against him.

"Ivan, it is you, it is *you*!" she cried. "I just cannot believe it."

The Duke put his arm round her.

"We are in a hurry," he said loudly enough for the Equerry to overhear, "and we have to leave immediately. The carriage is outside."

Even as he spoke, the double doors were opened up and then, taking Devinia by the hand, he drew her down the steps.

He pushed her into the carriage and told the driver in his own language to go to the Port as quick as possible.

Then he shook the Equerry by the hand and got into the carriage pulling the door closed behind him before the servant could do so.

As the carriage then started to move, Devinia flung herself against him.

"You have come! *You have come*!" she cried out breathlessly. "I never thought – you would find me. Oh, how are you – here?"

There were tears in her eyes and at the same time they were shining.

As the Duke put his arms round her, she seemed to melt against him.

Then, as his lips found hers and he kissed her, he knew, as he did so, that this was the greatest moment of his life.

He loved her as he had never loved anyone before.

They had gone quite a way before Devinia gave a gasp and whispered,

"You have come and – I thought I was lost – for ever."

"Of course, I followed you once I knew what had happened," the Duke replied. "Now you are safe and I will never let you go again."

"Hold me," she cried. "I have been – so frightened and so terrified and now like a miracle you are here! How can you be so clever? How could you have saved me when I thought that – no one would be able to do so?"

She was speaking excitedly and was almost in tears.

As he had no words to express his own anxiety, the Duke could only kiss her and keep on kissing her so that neither of them could speak.

Only as they reached the Port did Devinia say,

"I must look very strange, but you do realise that I have no clothes except these I am wearing."

"We will buy you plenty of clothes when we reach Athens," the Duke promised.

"Are we going to – Greece?" Devinia asked him excitedly. "I would love that!"

"I thought that you would want to be married there rather than anywhere else," the Duke said quietly.

Her eyes opened wide and she stared at him.

"*Married*!" she whispered.

At that moment the carriage came to a standstill on the quay and the Duke's yacht was there waiting for them.

The Duke stepped out of the carriage and paid the driver and, when he was ready to board, he helped Devinia out of the carriage and up the gangway.

The Captain was waiting for them on the deck.

If he was surprised at Devinia's appearance, he was too polite to show it.

"Move out to sea as quickly as you can," the Duke ordered.

"Aye, aye, Your Grace", the Captain saluted.

Devinia, more to hide her appearance than because she wanted to sit down, had moved into the Saloon and the Duke followed her.

"Is there anything I can get you, Your Grace?" one of the Stewards asked him.

"We would both love a glass of champagne," the Duke told him. "We have won a great victory and we want to celebrate it."

The Steward smiled.

"Very good, Your Grace."

He disappeared and Devinia slipped her hand into the Duke's.

"How could you have been – so clever?" she asked. "How could you have been so wonderful as to find me? I prayed all the way here that you would read my thoughts and would know where I had been taken."

"Forget it," the Duke said. "You are free now and you are mine. To make quite certain you cannot escape me again, we are going to be married, as I have already told you, as soon as we reach Athens."

"I thought you might have been – joking," Devinia murmured.

"I have never been more serious. But there is one thing I want to know. Are you marrying me for my title or because I am me?"

Devinia wanted to laugh, but instead she replied,

"I have loved you for a long time, but I thought you did not want to marry – anyone."

"I never wanted to marry anyone until I met you. But I can think of no better way of keeping you safe."

He smiled at her as he added,

"Unless you really dislike the idea, I suggest we are married either by the Captain at sea or as soon as we reach Athens."

"*I love you*," Devinia whispered. "I have loved you for such a long time, but I thought, as we were only having a pretend engagement, you would be angry if I fell in love with you – so I was determined to hide it."

"I will tell you about my love, but I want to hear about yours," the Duke said. "First we need to be sustained after what we have been through. Also we have to drink to the happiness of our marriage."

He kissed her cheek before he added,

"A marriage that neither of us expected, but which I know is going to be a perfect one. A Heaven on Earth."

Devinia gave a murmur of happiness.

As she did so, the Steward arrived with a bottle of champagne and poured out two glasses.

Then, as he left the Saloon, closing the door behind him, Devinia slipped her hand into the Duke's again.

"I love you! I love you!" she sighed. "But I am so afraid I will – bore you by telling you so."

"I want you to tell me every moment and I want you just as you are and I love you as I have never loved anyone before. I thought when I lost you that I had lost everything that mattered and nothing I was or possessed was of any consequence because you were not with me."

He spoke with a deep sincerity that she could not misunderstand.

Because she was so happy she hid her face against his shoulder.

"I love you! I adore you!" she whispered. "I feel that this is all a dream and I will wake up to find I am still a prisoner."

"If you wake up anywhere, it will be in my arms," the Duke answered, "and just as you love me, I love you as I never thought it possible to love anyone. I hope never again to go through the agony I had when I realised what had happened to you and that I might not be able to save you."

"I lay awake all last night," she answered, "thinking how I could die and knowing it was impossible because in the harem they do not even have table knives in case a girl tried to use one – on herself."

"Forget it! Forget it!" the Duke said firmly. "It was all a terrible mistake which should never have happened in the first place. But it made me realise now much you meant to me and the only way I can protect you is by making you my wife."

"I will try to do everything – you want me to do," Devinia promised. "But you must not be bored if I go on saying, I love you! I love you!"

She just managed to say the last words before the Duke was kissing her again.

Kissing her until the engines began turning beneath them and she knew that they were leaving Turkey.

That they were sailing into a Heaven of their own, which would be unlike anything that had ever happened to either of them before.

*

When they reached Athens, it was very nearly three o'clock in the afternoon.

The Duke told Devinia that he wanted her to visit the Church where they were to be married as he knew the Priest in charge.

"I must have something decent to wear," Devinia said. "Anyone seeing me would be horrified at the lowness and transparency of this dress I am wearing."

"You look lovely," he told her. "But I understand what you are feeling and we will stop at the shop in the town which has the best clothes in Athens."

Devinia borrowed from the Captain a shawl which he had worn when he had a cold and it at least covered her shoulders.

She and the Duke drove off in a covered carriage and it was not very far to the shop he had told her about.

The first thing she noticed when she climbed out of the carriage was that in the window they were exhibiting the most beautiful Wedding dress that she had ever seen.

It was on a wooden model and she could not help thinking that it was just by luck or perhaps a gift from the Gods that it should be there at this particular moment.

As she and the Duke walked to the door, she said,

"I want that Wedding dress! I want it because it is the prettiest one I have seen and I want you to remember our Wedding as I will for the rest of our lives."

"Then, of course, you shall have it," he replied.

Inside he told the owner that his fiancée had been unfortunate to have had her entire trousseau stolen while she was in one of the Eastern countries.

"So we have come here to supply her with a new trousseau and most of all she wants the Wedding dress in the window."

The owner was silent for a while and then he said,

"I will do my very best to supply the beautiful lady with everything she requires, but there is already a lady hesitating as to whether she will buy the Wedding dress or not and she is going to let me know this evening."

"I will let you know now," Devinia said. "If it fits me, which I am sure it will, I will take it with me."

And turning to the Duke she said,

"I think it would be wisest if they took the dresses and the other clothes I need to the yacht tomorrow. I can then try them on without boring you."

The Duke smiled and she went on,

"However I do need a dress to wear now," and both the Duke and the owner thought that this was an excellent idea.

The owner took Devinia into a changing room and one of his saleswomen produced three pretty dresses which they were sure would fit her.

She chose one in a very soft shade of blue because she knew it would match her eyes and make her fair hair look even lovelier.

She made up her mind quickly and did not bother to try on the other dresses.

"Please take them to the yacht," she said. "I don't want to bore my fiancé by waiting for me while I try on dresses here."

She then told them she needed underclothes and pretty nightgowns as well.

"In fact, a whole trousseau," she insisted, "as I have nothing except this dress that I wore last night for a Fancy Dress Ball."

"I wondered why you were wearing it, madam," one of the saleswomen piped up.

"It was only when we arrived back where we were staying that we found everything had gone," she went on. "You can imagine how upset I was."

"So we will make you the most beautiful trousseau any bride has ever had," the saleswoman promised.

Devinia, however, was thinking of just how boring this was for the Duke.

She had known all her life that men always found that women shopping were tiresome.

The mere fact they could not make up their mind over which article they were buying made them say, as her father had once, that he would never go shopping again.

When she joined the Duke, he had actually left the shop and was talking to a man outside about the horses he owned. He was telling the Duke where he had bought them and the price he had paid for them.

Devinia said quickly,

"I am finished and I have everything with me."

The saleswoman was just behind her carrying the Wedding dress in a large box.

"Did you put in the veil?" Devinia asked as she suddenly remembered that she had not seen her doing so.

"Yes, it is there safely and I promise you, madam, you will not be disappointed. It is the most beautiful dress we have ever had in our shop, as quite a number of ladies have told us."

Devinia thought that she was extremely fortunate in finding a Wedding dress that she really loved.

The Duke helped her into the carriage and he told the coachman to take them to the Church.

As they drove off, the Duke commented,

"You are the fastest shopper I have ever known and I cannot believe anyone has ever managed to buy an entire trousseau in less than fifteen minutes!"

"Men are always bored with women who fuss about their clothes," Devinia said. "That is what Papa told me and Mama was very careful never to make him wait for her if she was out shopping."

"As I have thought you have been extremely well brought up," the Duke remarked. "But I want you, my darling, to have everything you want, even if I do have to wait for it."

"At the moment I have you and that is everything I want," Devinia whispered.

"And I can say the same. Now, I want you to be as delighted with this Church as I was when I first saw it. I think you will understand how much it means to me when I tell you it was built on a site which once held a Temple of Aphrodite."

Devinia gave a cry.

"She was the Goddess of Love."

"That is what I was told," the Duke replied. I think you will find, as I did, that it is and always will be a place which inspires love."

Devinia was fascinated.

"You must give me a book all about it," she said, "and, of course, as you told me how much Greece means to you, it is only right that it is where we should be married."

"I thought when I was last here that if I was ever going to marry I would bring the woman I love here."

His voice deepened as he carried on,

"Because this is the country of love, I felt so deeply moved by everything I saw and love seemed to be in the very air itself."

Devinia was about to speak when he said,

"That is why I know, if we are married here today, our love will be blessed by the Goddess of Love and by God Himself and it will last for ever."

He spoke in a serious tone which Devinia had not heard before, but felt deeply moved by his words.

Because she could not think of how to express her feelings, she bent and kissed his hand which he had on his knee.

"I love you! I love you!" she said. "I just know that every minute of every day and every year we are together, I will love you more and more."

The Duke put his arm round her and pulled her close to him.

For a moment, as what she had just said seemed to be ringing on the air, they were silent.

When she saw the Church, Devinia knew at once why it had meant so much to the Duke.

It was very old and beautiful.

It had maybe been built by the same craftsmen who had built the Temples for the Gods.

There were endless flowers round the outside of it.

When she then entered it, she felt at once a strange sensation which was different from anything she had ever known before.

The Church was relatively small, but the altar was exceedingly beautiful and the Cross and the six candles on it were of shining gold.

There was an old Priest walking down the aisle.

When he saw the Duke, he stopped and the pleasure in his eyes was very obvious.

It was the Duke who spoke first.

"I promised you, Father, I would come back," he said, "and here I am. I hope you have not forgotten me."

"But naturally I have not forgotten you," the Priest replied. "I have often thought of you and prayed that you would found what you were seeking."

"Only you, Father, knew just what I was seeking," the Duke replied. "But I have found her when I was certain that my searching was impossible and now I want you to marry us tomorrow morning."

"I can imagine nothing I want to do more than to marry you," the old Priest said. "But I have a very large funeral tomorrow morning and so it would be better if you were married today."

The Duke turned and gazed at Devinia.

"Why not?" he asked.

For a moment she did not reply and then she said almost in a whisper,

"Please, I do so want – to wear the Wedding dress we have just bought."

The Duke looked at the Priest.

"I am sure, Father, that your wife would allow her to change in your house which I know is only next door."

"Of course," he replied. "She would be delighted as she too has often spoken about you and wondered if 'that handsome boy' as she called you, had ever got married."

"The answer was 'no' until this moment," the Duke answered, "and that is just why, Father, I have brought my future wife here, the moment my yacht came into Port."

"If that is where you are," the Priest replied, "then there is no reason for you to go back. Your fiancée can change in my house and my wife will be pleased to help."

He smiled before he added,

"I must find my two sons who will take part in your Wedding, who can help me prepare the Church."

The Duke merely nodded and the Priest went on,

"It is now, I think, getting on for five o'clock. If you are married at six o'clock, which is usually the time we close the Church, there will be no visitors and you two young people will have the place to yourselves."

"That is what I want," the Duke replied. "I have always been afraid of being forced into a large Wedding. I can imagine that nothing could be more perfect than if you marry Devinia and me here alone."

Devinia thought that, if he had ended his sentence, he would have said 'except for the Gods'.

But she understood how deeply he felt about this lovely little Church and she slipped her hand into his and said,

"This is what I want too and it is something that we will always remember."

"Of course, we will," the Duke agreed.

"You know the way to my house," the Priest said, "and now I will get busy and make the Church look as beautiful for you as is possible."

"You know, Father, that I don't need to express my gratitude," the Duke told him, "but you are aware how truly grateful I am."

Then, taking Devinia by the arm, he led her out of the little Church and along the path outside to where, set in a garden, was a small but enchanting house.

A maid let them in and after they were shown into an attractive sitting room, the Priest's wife came in.

She had aged a great deal, the Duke thought, since he had last seen her and her hair was completely white, but she still had the English look of a Lady of Quality.

When she held out both hands to him, he took them in his and kissed them one after another.

"You have not forgotten me?" he asked.

"Of course not," she answered. "I often wondered how you were getting on and if you had ever married. As you told my husband it was something you would not do until you were older."

"It was a vow I made because I felt that no woman could in any way be as attractive as the glorious Goddesses of Greece," the Duke replied. "But now I have found what I was seeking and your husband is marrying us in an hour."

The Priest's wife gave a cry of delight.

"What we are asking you is if Devinia could change into her Wedding dress here, as I now understand that your husband has a funeral tomorrow morning, which was when we asked to be married."

"So, you are to be married tonight!" she exclaimed. "Oh, that is much better! There are always holidaymakers poking their noses in and tonight you can have the Church all to yourself."

"That is exactly what we want," the Duke agreed. "And I am hoping that the Wedding dress will fit Devinia."

"If it does not I will sew it on her!"

She took Devinia into a pretty bedroom and helped her change into the Wedding dress from the shop window.

It looked, she thought, even more enchanting on her than it had in the shop window and what was more the saleswoman was right, it fitted her exactly.

The veil covered her hair and fell down over her face.

"What you must have," the Priest's wife said, "is a halo of flowers. Your hair is so lovely but it will, of course, be hidden until you throw back the veil after the ring has been put on your finger."

Devinia was only too willing to let her arrange her hair as she wished.

She then disappeared into the garden to come back with a large number of small white roses for the garland of flowers for Devinia's hair.

She said, however, she could not bear to hide the beauty of her hair underneath the veil so Devinia gave her permission to cut the veil in half so that it fell on either side of her face.

"You are too pretty, my dear, to hide your face and I know that the Duke will want to look at you while you make your vows and so will my husband. He has never liked veils which hide from him what he wants to see."

"What is that?" Devinia asked her.

"He wants to see that what you say is the truth that comes from your soul and that you love the man you are marrying so that it shows in your eyes."

"You are so right, that is what you should show," Devinia said, "and I love the Duke with all my heart and soul."

The Priest's wife kissed her.

"That is what I want you to say. I thought when I first met him he was a very clever and unusual man who loved Greece. As he said, it gave him something he had always sought but believed he would never find."

Devinia thought that it was what she wanted herself but she was too shy to say so.

It was five minutes to six, when the Duke who was waiting for them downstairs, told them the time.

"We must go to the Church," he urged.

Devinia came down from the bedroom where she had changed.

The Duke took one look at her and thought it would be impossible for any woman to look so lovely.

"Even the Goddesses will pay their homage to you tonight," he said very softly so that only she could hear.

"So do I look as you want me to look?" Devinia whispered.

"As I hope and prayed my wife would look when I found her," the Duke replied. "Now I have found her I can only tell you that you are perfect in every way. Not only with your amazing beauty but because you have given me your heart."

"It is yours, completely and absolutely yours," she answered.

They walked a short way to the Church and, as they drew nearer, they heard the organ playing.

"The two boys have been helping their father," the Duke said, "to arrange the Church and one of them always plays the organ when there is a Service."

When they went through the Church door, Devinia gave a gasp.

In their absence someone, and Devinia thought that it must be the sons of the Priest, had put flowers in every window and in the centre of them was a lit candle.

There were also flowers all over the altar.

As the six candles were lit the whole place seemed to vibrate with beauty and the strange feeling of Holiness which she had known when she first entered.

Wearing his Vestments, the Priest was waiting for them and, as they walked slowly up the aisle towards him, the organ was playing softly.

The Service was short but the way the Priest read it made it seem just as if an Archangel himself was marrying them.

When they made their vows, Devinia was sure that her mother was looking down at her and she was happy and content that she had found a man who loved her as much as she loved him.

'I love him! I love him!' Devinia thought to herself when she knelt to pray.

Then, as the Priest blessed them, she was sure that she and Ivan were receiving the Blessing of all the angels of Heaven.

As well they were being blessed by the Gods and Goddesses of Greece who had lived and brought the secret of love to the world.

When the Service was over, Devinia and the Duke climbed into their carriage and drove away.

"It was a wonderful, wonderful Service," Devinia said. "I did not have time to thank the Priest."

"But I did," the Duke answered. "I gave him a large sum of money which I knew he would give to the Church. I gave a present for his wife and his children too, which he will enjoy as much as they will."

Devinia moved nearer to him.

"You are marvellous," she sighed. "You think of everything."

"I think of you," he said and took Devinia's hand in his.

They were silent.

And it seemed as if the Holiness of the Service had carried them into another world.

A world where there was only love and it was quite impossible to think or feel anything else but love.

The moon and the stars were coming out when they reached the yacht.

It was because of the Duke's orders, Devinia learnt later, that there was no one waiting for them.

The Duke drew Devinia into the Saloon where their dinner was laid out for them and there was champagne in a gold ice-cooler.

In the centre of the table was a cake iced in white with their initials engraved on it and encircled with white roses.

There were flowers everywhere on the whole yacht making a kaleidoscope of intense colour.

"It is all so lovely!" Devinia exclaimed. "How did you manage to arrange all this to make me so happy?"

"I sent a messenger to the yacht while you were dressing yourself in your Wedding gown and the Captain has followed my instructions as I knew he would."

"Did you tell him that we were being married?" she asked.

"I told him we would be married when we returned and that we wished to see no one," the duke replied. "The crew are drinking our health in champagne."

"I must thank the chef tomorrow for what he has produced for us in such a short time," Devinia told him.

The Duke nodded his agreement.

"How can you be so wonderful as to think of everything that makes me so happy?" Devinia asked.

"I love you," the Duke answered. "And we will spend our honeymoon here in Greece where the Gods have brought love to the world that will last for millions of years."

"I love you with all my heart and my soul, Ivan, but I am so afraid that it is not enough for you."

"It is all I want," the Duke replied. "I know that our love will go on increasing day by day and year by year."

"We must be sure – of that," Devinia whispered.

Then the Duke was kissing her.

Kissing her lips gently at first and then wildly and demandingly and passionately as if he was afraid of losing her again.

When the Duke finally made her his, she knew that they had both found a Heaven of Love that would always be theirs.

'I love you! *I love you*!" Devinia sighed softly.

She felt, as the Duke pulled her ever closer to him, that she had never been happier.

"I love you so very much, my darling Devinia," he breathed. "You are mine now and for ever."

The flowers whispered the same message and the stars shining through the porthole said it too.

"I love you! I love you!"

The love they had found together on this earth came from God, was part of God and was theirs for Eternity and even beyond.